# The Crystal Palace

The Talisman - Book V

# The Crystal Palace

Michael Harling

*iv*

Lindenwald ⊥P Press

*To Mitch and Charlie*
*Without whom there would be no story.*

Also by Michael Harling

The Postcards Trilogy
*Postcards From Across the Pond*
*More Postcards From Across the Pond*
*Postcards From Ireland*

The Talisman Series
*The Magic Cloak*
*The Roman Villa*
*The Sacred Tor*
*The Bard of Tilbury*

*Finding Rachel Davenport*

# Chapter 1
## Saturday, 8 July 2017

## Mitch

"Is she out there again?" Charlie asked, striding into my room.

I flipped a page in the book I was reading and nodded. "Like clockwork."

Charlie went to the window and looked out. "Every morning. Every single morning since summer began. Rain or shine."

"Yup. Like clockwork."

"And you're sure today is the day?"

I put my book down and went to the window to stand next to Charlie. It was a clear morning. The grass in the yard was dewy and long. Dad would want me to cut it soon. Mom was there, reclining on a chaise lounge she had dragged from the back porch. A patio table sat next to her. On it was a cup of coffee. Empty. She was reading, holding the book with one hand while the other unconsciously pulled strands of hair from the back of her head, a habit she acquired every year as summer approached.

"As sure as I can be," I said.

"And what if you're wrong?"

I shrugged. "Then I'm wrong. And we try again."

"But she'll get suspicious if we do it too often."

"Then we'll have to hope that I'm right." I looked

at my watch. "It's getting close. We'd better go.

We went downstairs, hoping to avoid Dad, who was in the kitchen making breakfast. But as I put my hand on the back door, he called to us.

"Where're you going, boys? Breakfast is nearly ready."

I stopped but kept my hand on the doorknob. "Just for a walk."

Yeah," Charlie said. "It's a nice morning. We won't be long."

Dad came to the kitchen door, wearing the pink, frilly apron Mom keeps on a hook next to the refrigerator. I wasn't sure if he wanted me to laugh or not. I chose not.

"Why don't you ask your mom to go with you?" he said. "I think she's still out front."

"Um, I'm pretty sure she'd rather stay out there," Charlie said.

I nodded. "She says she's relaxing."

Dad rubbed his chin. "I suppose you're right. She's been on edge lately. Maybe you should leave her."

"Sure Dad," I said, pushing the door open. "We won't disturb her."

"But don't go far. Breakfast in ten minutes."

Outside, we ran across our neighbour's yard, and then the next, hoping they were all still in bed, or at least not looking out their back doors. Then we went to the road, ambling away from our house, trying not to seem as if we were waiting for the mail truck, and the mailman, Mr. Levin, who would, hopefully, have a package for us.

Every year about this time, one of Granddad's gifts—the key to our adventure—arrives. And even though she can't know what that means, Mom always

2

tries to keep the cloak—the vehicle to our adventure—from us. We think it has to do with the cloak being the first gift, and her holding a grudge because Granddad ran off to England, or something. Anyway, she kept trying to take the cloak, but last year Dad made her give it to us. So, this year, she started getting up early and parking herself in the front yard to wait for the mailman. Both Charlie and I thought that meant she was planning to take the gift from us instead of the cloak. And we weren't going to allow that.

Her problem was, she didn't know when the gift would come. All she knew was that it arrived on a seemingly random date in the early part of our summer vacation, which was why she had to camp out by the mailbox every morning. But I knew, or thought I knew, the exact day.

"There he is," Charlie said, pointing toward a small truck, stopping next to a mailbox three houses down the road. "Should we run and stop him?"

I shook my head. "No. Just go to the next mailbox. We'll meet him there."

"But what if they don't have any mail today?"

"We'll worry about that if it happens."

"And what if you're wrong about this moon thing?"

I shrugged. "Then I'm wrong. But there's a full moon tonight, and all the other gifts arrived on the day of the full moon. I don't see why this one should be any different." We reached the next mailbox and stopped. "Besides, it's too late to change our minds now."

The white and blue truck slowed as it approached, stopping at the mailbox. The driver, wearing a non-regulation tee shirt with an AC-DC logo on it, leaned out the window, pulled the front flap open and stuffed an envelope inside.

"Good morning, Mr. Levin," I said.

Mr. Levin closed the mailbox. "Hello. You're Tom Wyman's twins. What brings you out here?"

"We're not twins," I said.

"Yeah," Charlie added, "but we are the same age."

I sighed. Charlie never failed to mention that. "Only for a few weeks," I said. "I'll be older than him in August."

Mr. Levin nodded and put the truck in gear. "Then you're what my dear old gran would call Irish Twins."

"Do you have any mail for us?" I called, as he started to pull away.

The truck stopped, and Mr. Levin shuffled through a pile of mail on the passenger's seat. "I have a few bills for your father, and there's a package here for you."

Charlie jumped forward. "Can we have it."

"Oh, I don't know. That might be against regulations, handing mail out willy-nilly to boys loitering along the road."

"But it's for us," Charlie said.

I stepped up beside him. "We won't tell anyone."

Mr. Levin smiled. "Well, I suppose I can make an exception this time." He leaned out, holding a few envelopes and a small package in his hand.

Charlie grabbed the package. "You can give those to mom. She's, you know, waiting for you. I think she likes to get the mail."

Mr. Levin's smile faltered as he returned the envelopes to the pile. "Yes. She's been waiting for me every morning for weeks. Very … dedicated of her."

4

I waved and stepped back, pulling Charlie with me. "Thanks, Mr. Levin."

The truck lurched. Mr. Levin gave us a quick wave and drove away.

"Well, we got the gift," I said, looking at the package in Charlie's hand. It was small, not even in a box, just a brown, padded envelope.

"Should we open it?"

"Not now," I said. "No time. Dad'll be looking for us, and Mom will be inside now that she's got the mail."

Charlie nodded, watching as the truck trundled toward our house. "Let's hope he doesn't tell her anything."

He rolled the envelope and stuffed it in his pocket, and we returned the way we had come, arriving just as Dad—thankfully, no longer wearing the apron—came to the back door to call us. Inside, Mom was already at the dining room table, the envelopes Mr. Levin had given her stacked neatly beside her plate. She smiled as we sat, waiting for Dad to bring in the pancakes and bacon.

The meal went well. There was the usual, casual conversation—Dad mentioned that the front lawn needed mowing, Charlie said he needed to be at ball practice that afternoon—and I began to relax. Then Mom picked up one of the envelopes and began opening it, slowly, while looking at me.

"The mailman says he saw you this morning."

I felt my face go white. I hoped she didn't notice, but I was certain she did. "Yes. We were walking, and we saw him."

She lifted the flap of the envelope, pulled out the paper that was inside, unfolded it and placed it aside without looking at it. "And …?"

"And he gave us a package," Charlie said, "that was addressed to us."

Mom pushed her plate away and leaned forward. "Give it to me."

My jaw dropped. "What!"

Charlie folded his arms. "No!"

Dad held his head in his hands. "Dear God!"

Mom let the silence hang for a few seconds, then she glared at Charlie. "What did you say to me, Charles?"

Charlie didn't miss a beat. "I said, 'No.' It's addressed to us. It's ours. Why should we give it to you?"

"As punishment," she said. "You went behind my back. You purposely stopped the mailman—"

Charlie's chair made a screeching noise as he stood up, his hands balled into fists at his side. "We did not!"

"You did! And you knew it was wrong. If it wasn't, you wouldn't feel guilty about it." She looked directly at me. "And you do feel guilty, don't you?"

I sat up, my eyes wide, staring at her in disbelief. She was right, about everything—we did go behind her back, and I did feel guilty about it—but she was slanting it, making our wrong into her right. It wasn't fair, and I knew why it wasn't fair, but was this the time for truth? I looked at Charlie. He was getting ready to say something, and I figured the truth would be better than whatever he had in mind.

"I don't feel guilty," I said, my voice rising. "I feel sad. Sad that we had to get to Mr. Levin first, because if he had given the package to you, you wouldn't have allowed us to have it. Tell me that's not true."

Dad slammed his hand on the table, making me jump. "Enough," he said. "Enough, already."

Mom ignored him. "Open it," she said. "Right now. Show me what it is."

I looked at Charlie. He shrugged, pulled the envelope from his pocket and sat back down.

When he ripped it open, a slip of paper fell out, along with two metal objects that clanged on the tabletop.

"What are they?" Mom asked.

Charlie looked at them and shook his head. "I don't know."

I didn't, either. They were identical, about as long as a toothbrush and, in a heavy, metallic way, sorta looked like toothbrushes. The handle was tapered, and tipped with a marble-sized ball, and at the other end, four, stout metal stumps, uniform in size and shape, stood in for bristles. At the very tip, at the base of the bristles, was a small metal wheel. Whatever they were, they had at one time been red, but the paint was faded and dulled with age, and showing patches of bare metal.

I picked up the paper. It was, as I suspected, a letter from Granddad, though it was less of a letter and more of a quick note and didn't tell me much. "I took another visit to the What-Not shop that old man runs and found these," it read. "I thought you might find them interesting. Love, Granddad."

I saw Mom was looking at me. "Well? What are they?"

I shook my head. "He doesn't say, and I don't know."

Mom stretched out her hand. "Then they might be dangerous. Give them to me."

Charlie grabbed them and held them in his fist.

"You can't—"

"I can!"

"They're glass cutters," Dad said.

Mom lowered her hand. "What?"

"Glass cutters. Old fashioned ones. For cutting old fashion glass."

"Then they are dangerous," Mom said.

"No, they're not," Dad said, his voice loud enough to startle me. He stood. "And I have an idea. There's some glass in the cellar. Come with me, boys, I'll show you how they work."

Mom looked at Dad, her eyes wide. "But they can't—"

"They can." Dad said, as he walked away.

We hurried after him.

# Chapter 2

## Charlie

I felt a huge sense of relief as I closed the cellar door and descended the stairs behind Dad and Mitch. From the dining room, I heard the sound of clanking, as Mom cleared the table with such vigour I was afraid she'd break the dishes.

Dad threw the main switch, replacing the murky glow of the stairway light with brilliant white. I shielded my eyes as I took the final steps, while Dad and Mitch moved tools and cuts of wood from the scarred workbench.

"So, what do these do?" I asked, dropping the things Granddad had sent us onto the cleared area.

"They're glass cutters," Dad said. "They cut glass. What did you think they'd do?"

He wasn't as jolly as he usually was when he showed us stuff. He wasn't smiling; he was grimacing.

"I've got some glass around somewhere," he said, yanking open drawers and checking inside an old cabinet. When he found what he was looking for, he brought it to the workbench: four panes of dust-coated glass, about a foot long and eight inches wide. He dusted off an area of the bench top and laid one of the pieces on it.

"This is old glass," he said. "Nowadays they use double-paned windows with thermal glass. You wouldn't be able to cut those. But these came from windows that were originally in the house, so your cutters should work on them."

Mitch picked up one of the glass cutters and examined it. "How?"

Dad pulled a metal ruler from beneath a jumble of tools, laid it on the glass and took the cutter from Mitch. "Like this."

He held the ruler with one hand and set the tiny wheel of the cutter on the glass. "You have to press hard, but not so hard you break it." It made a low screeching sound, like fingernails on a blackboard, as he pulled it along the ruler, leaving a bright scar on the glass. Then he lifted the glass and slid the ruler underneath it, just beyond the line he had made.

"Now," he said, turning the cutter around, "you give it a light tap."

The glass made a ping sound when he hit it with the ball, and the windowpane snapped in two, leaving a clean, straight break.

"Wow," Mitch said. "Can I try?"

Dad handed him the cutter and Mitch took one of the half panes.

"Press a bit harder," Dad said. "You need to score it good."

When Mitch tapped it with the ball, the glass cracked.

"Not bad for a first effort," Dad said. "Try again."

Then the cellar door opened, and Mom yelled down. "You can keep your toys, but since you went behind my back, I'm taking the cloak." Then she slammed the door.

Mitch, in mid-cut, stopped and laid the cutter down. I rolled my eyes and sighed. Dad just shook his head.

"Look," he said, "I don't know what your mother's issue is, but can't you—"

I held up my cutter. "This is ours. The cloak is ours. She can't take them from us."

"And what she said about us going behind her back," Mitch said, "that's not true. We simply picked up a package that was for us. That's all."

"You pre-empted her, then," Dad said. "Because you suspected she might not let you have it."

"No," I said. "We didn't suspect; we knew. And we were right. What's she's doing is irrational."

"I'd say, 'Not fair,'" Mitch said, probably thinking I'd stepped over a line. Turns out he was right.

Dad glared at me. "Irrational? Irrational is wanting to play with a cloak every year after my dad's gifts arrive, when you ignore it the other eleven months. Your mother is right about one thing, you are getting too old for that."

Mitch spoke before I could think of a way to answer.

"It's ours, and it doesn't matter when we want to play with it, or why. But we want it now because it's a tradition. Granddad sent us the cloak at the beginning of summer, and now he sends us random gifts. It all seems connected, the cloak, the gifts, summer vacation, and Granddad. We haven't seen him since we were seven. I don't know if this is his way of staying close to us, but I do know it's our way of staying close to him. So, what's the harm in having the gifts, and the cloak, at the same time?"

Dad sighed. "I don't … she's not … if only you hadn't gone behind her back."

"We didn't go behind her back," I said. "We—"

11

Dad held up his hand. "That's not how she sees it."

"But it's the truth."

"Look, I'll do what I can. Will that satisfy you?"

I nodded.

"Yes," Mitch said. "And thanks, Dad."

Dad sighed again, then he turned and headed up the stairs, taking slow, deliberate steps, like a man on his way to the gallows.

"That was a good move," I said, when I heard the thump of the cellar door closing, "bringing Granddad up. That's what got him on side."

Mitch turned back to the pane of glass and positioned the ruler. "Hopefully, it will be enough."

I cleared some more room on the workbench and laid one of the panes in it. "Gotta hope so. These cutters won't do us much good if she won't give us the cloak."

I scratched the glass with the cutter, without the help of the ruler, scoring a straight mark across one of the corners. Then I tapped it with the ball end of the cutter. It snapped clean, making a neat triangle.

Mitch tapped his, and the glass shattered. "Shit!"

I traced an arc on the pane with the cut corner. When I tapped it, I got a smooth, curved piece of glass. Then Mitch broke another piece.

Then I tried a circle, using a jar lid for a template. I traced it three times before I was confident it was cut deep enough. When I tapped it, a perfect circle popped out.

"This sucks," Mitch said.

I held up the glass circle I had made. "I didn't think this would be so easy."

Mitch threw his cutter on the work bench. "I'm

not sure what good it will do if we're not going to get to use them."

"Don't be like that" I said, "you just need to practice more."

"I don't know …"

Then we heard muffled shouts from upstairs.

We went to the stairs and crept up the steps, then sat close to the door so we could hear.

"They don't deserve it, that's why." Mom's voice. Shrill and loud. We didn't need to be sitting at the door to have heard it. "They went behind my back to get that package before I could. Their punishment is, they don't get the cloak."

"They saw the mail man and he gave them a package that belongs to them," Dad said, his voice straining at the edge of calm.

"You're splitting hairs; they set out to deceive me. They deserve to be punished."

"Okay. But why was it you wanted to get the package first. Were you planning to keep it from them, not let them know it came?"

"No," Mom said. Then her voice became less shrill. "I … I just—"

"You're just upset because they did an end run around you. You were going to keep that package from them. Why is that? What do you have against them playing with a cloak my father sent them?"

"It's just … Mitch will be seventeen in August. And Charlie's sixteen now. They're too old to be playing make-believe."

"They're not playing." Now Dad's voice grew strident. "They are trying to stay close to their grandfather, this is how they remember him. Why do you want to take that away from them? Punishment?

Too old? They're just lame excuses. What's the real reason? Is it my father? I know he's eccentric but that doesn't give you the right—"

"It changes them!" Mom shouted.

The silence lasted so long, I thought they might have left the room. Then I heard Dad's voice, quiet and tentative. "What?"

"I know you won't believe me," Mom said, her voice breaking. "But think about it. Mitch didn't want to try out for baseball, and as soon as they got the cloak, he changed his mind, and did well."

"That's just a coincidence. How can you—"

Mom kept on, her voice hitching and hiccupping as the words poured out of her. "And remember when we visited that farm, and the boys got the chance to ride horses, and they rode as if they'd been doing it all their lives? And last year, they got those feathers, and suddenly they could do somersaults and back flips."

"It's summer vacation, they're two growing boys, of course they're going to try new things, surprising things, that's got nothing to do with the cloak."

"It changes them. You can laugh at me, you can call me mad, but I know."

"Honey," Dad said, his voice quiet now, almost inaudible. "Let's say it does, okay, and that the reason they can do those things is because of the cloak. Is that any reason to not let them have it? It seems to me, it only does them good."

"But what if they don't come back this time?" Mother sobbed.

Mitch's eyes widened. I sat straight, straining my ears, but Dad said nothing.

"She knows," I whispered.

"She can't," Mitch said.

"Then why all the fuss?"

Mitch had no answer for that. He leaned his ear against the door again.

"Back?" Dad said, after about half a minute of silence. "Back from where?"

"What does it matter?" Mom was in full melt-down mode now. "You won't believe me, but it's dangerous. It's dangerous, I know it."

"Look, honey," Dad said, "I think we need to talk this through, but can't we just agree, for now, that maybe this is at least a little bit in your imagination? It's not as if Dad sent them a handgun; they're glass cutters, that's all. Nothing dangerous, I promise."

Mom sniffed. "What if he does send them something dangerous, will you agree with me to keep that cloak away from them?"

Another pause, not as long as the other. Then Dad caved. "Yes," he said. "I can agree to that."

More silence, then a chair scraped, and I heard slow, heavy footsteps.

"Let's go," Mitch whispered.

We went back to the workbench. Mitch cleared the broken glass and took one of the panes. I kept working on the one I had cut the circle from. I tried to concentrate, and not think about what might be happening upstairs.

A few minutes later, the cellar door opened, and Dad came down, holding the cloak, which was rolled into a ball. His face was grim, and I made an effort to show no signs of glee at having won.

Mitch, ever the diplomat, said, "Thanks, Dad. We really appreciate it."

Dad shoved the cloak into Mitch's arms. "I did it

this time because I thought it was the right thing to do. But we need to start taking this seriously. Your mother … I think she …"

"It's okay," Mitch said. "She's just upset."

"She'll be fine tomorrow," I added.

"Maybe," Father said. "But if this happens next year …"

Mitch shrugged. "We'll worry about it then."

Dad shook his head and headed for the stairs. "I suppose you're right."

I watched him go, his footsteps, once again, heavy on the risers.

"I feel guilty about Mom," Mitch said, after Dad closed the cellar door behind him. "This is all our fault. And now Dad thinks Mom's crazy."

"Well, what are we supposed to do? If we tried to tell them what is really happening, they'd think we were crazy."

"And if they believed us, they'd never let us have it."

I ran a hand over the blue velvet bundle in Mitch's arms. "You think so? Even if they believed us?"

"If they believed us? They'd be stupid to let us go. It's far too dangerous."

I looked at Mitch, suddenly realizing what we had decided. "Then why do we do it?"

Mitch shook his head and gazed at the cloak. "I think, because we know we have to."

# Chapter 3

## Mitch

We agreed to meet in Charlie's room at midnight, but when the hour struck, I stayed in bed. Mom was awake, I could feel it; she was awake, and waiting. So, I waited too, keeping my mind alert, as I had on those long nights of guard duty with Harold's army.

The boredom, coupled with the awareness that to sleep would mean death, came back to me, not in a wave, but like the tide—a slow but inexorable filling of my mind with all that had happened last year, and the years before that.

Though never forgotten, the details of our adventures faded throughout the year, but came back into focus once the gifts arrived, so that now, in addition to the memory of those lonely hours, the sights, smells and sounds of all the other nights and days I had spent, either in the actual past, or the vivid dreamy adventures that the cloak somehow took us on, seeped into my mind and became part of my consciousness: the feel of the galloping horse beneath me, the scents carried on the wind, the pain of practice combat, the horror of real combat, the cheers of the crowd, the screams of the dying.

The final thought snapped me awake. For a moment, I thought it was morning, but it was only the full moon, shining through my window. I lay still, letting the fear drain from my body. The bedside clock read 3:15. It was still night, and the house felt, at last, fully asleep.

I got up slowly, trying to keep the bedsprings from creaking. I was already dressed for travel, in jeans, sneakers and heavy shirt. Having no idea where we might be heading, I put on a light jacket, picked up the cloak and tiptoed into the hallway. All was dark, still and silent. I went into Charlie's room and found him asleep, which was fine. More than fine, really. It would make things go quicker, I hoped. He was already dressed for travel, and had, I hoped, emptied his pockets, just as I had. We didn't know if anything would come with us. Usually it was only us, our clothes and the most recent gift, but we didn't want to take the chance of carrying a watch, cell phone, or money from the 21st century into the past.

I laid next to Charlie, slow and easy, being careful to not wake him, and spread the cloak over us.

There was only time to briefly wonder where we might end up this time before, I too, fell asleep.

# Chapter 4
## Thursday, 24 April 1851

## Charlie

"Vagabonds!"

An explosion of pain snapped me awake. I gripped my side and moaned.

"Wastrels!"

Another shock, this time to my shoulder. Then light from a low sun blinded me as the cloak flew into the air. I shielded my eyes and shook my head to clear away the confusion and pain. Standing above me, a man wearing dark clothes and an angry expression aimed a heavily booted foot at my face.

"Tramps!"

I ducked and rolled. The boot hit Mitch, instead. "Hey!" Mitch sprang to his feet. "Cut it!"

"Beggars! Thieves!"

Me and Mitch stood together and backed slowly away as the man—who was dressed in a fine, dark suit that hung loosely on his skinny frame—advanced on us. Rage contorted his thin face and spittle flew from his lips as he continued to shout at us. "No thieving vagrants on my land! Get off!" He swung his arm, the one not clutching our cloak. "Off now or I'll have the law on you."

He leapt forward, his fist raised. We darted in opposite directions, leaving the man standing between

19

us, fuming.

"Hey, we're leaving!" Mitch said. "Just give us … give that back and we'll go."

"And we're not thieves," I said.

"Oh, no?" The man held up the cloak. "You surely stole this."

"That's ours," I said. "Give it back!"

"Liars as well as thieves," the man said, clutching the cloak in his fists. "No vagabond owns a garment as fine as this."

"We're not vagabonds," Mitch said. "Just give it back and we'll leave, okay?"

"Not as I breathe," the man said, rolling the cloak and hugging it to his chest. "I'll see you in the cells for this. And in the stocks for your impertinence."

He turned from us and began walking toward a nearby farmhouse. Mitch looked at me. "I'm not losing the cloak. Not again."

I nodded. It would mean trouble, but we had no choice. Mitch ran toward the man. "No!" he shouted. "You give that back."

"It belongs to us," I yelled, running after him.

Mitch got to the man first and grabbed the cloak, but the man kicked and pushed. I jumped him from behind, making him stumble, but he turned and swung his arm at me as he fell.

Then I found myself lying on the ground, my head throbbing, my ears ringing, and my eyes trying to focus. I struggled to remember where I was. The short, leafy plants I was sprawled out on were wet with dew. The ground was soft. It looked like a field. A man, tall and skinny, stood over me.

"Wastrels!" The man sputtered.

I put a hand to my head and felt blood. How could

a skinny man like him pack such a powerful punch? He looked down at me, the cloak in one hand and a stout, black stick in the other. I tried to concentrate on the stick. It seemed a strange thing to have.

"You thought two strong lads against a single man would be an easy fight." He raised the stick above his head, and I saw it wasn't a stick at all, but a sort of leather sack. "I keep this cosh to hand for unruly tenants, but it can teach the likes of you a thing or two, as well."

I watched his arm, and the black sack, descend toward my face, then someone jerked me sideways. I heard a whoosh as the cosh missed my cheek by inches.

"C'mon, Charlie!"

It was Mitch, holding my arm and shouting in my face. The man was behind him, coming closer.

Mitch pulled me further away, trying to drag me to my feet as the man advanced.

"Charlie!" Mitch shouted, his voice distant, even though he was right next to me. He held my arm, watching the man who was almost upon us. "Remember what we did last year? With Ellen? To get away from the gang?"

I looked at Mitch. "I … yeah … I think …"

The man, close now, raised his arm.

"Break!" Mitch shouted. Then he pushed me away and ran.

I stumbled but kept on my feet. The man chased after Mitch, who kept dodging and staying just out of his reach. I drew a breath and began to remember. As nimbly as I could, I stayed behind the man, dodging with him, trying to guess Mitch's next move. Then, as the man swung for Mitch, I dropped to my hands and

21

knees, and hoped.

Mitch dove for the man, catching him off balance, and pushed him back. Before he had a chance to bring the cosh down on Mitch's head, they both tumbled over me. Mitch landed on top of the man, then he jumped up. "C'mon!"

I moved as fast as I could, grabbing up the cloak as I staggered past the man. But I jerked to a stop as the man gripped the cloak, clutching it with both hands. Mitch grabbed me, and the cloak, and pulled, but the man held firm. Then he began to get up.

Mitch let go and jumped at the man, knocking him flat, and landing on his chest. A whoosh of air came out of him, then he lay still, his eyes wide, his mouth opening and closing, gasping for breath like a beached mackerel. The cloak came loose.

"Go!" Mitch shouted.

I ran.

"No, this way."

I turned. Mitch had stopped in the field, not far away, and was kicking at the ground with the heel of his sneaker. "What are you doing?" I said, running toward him.

Mitch said nothing until I was next to him and saw he was digging a hole, and that he had taken the leather cosh from the man. Mitch dropped it into the shallow hole, filled it, then stomped it flat. "I'm marking our spot," he said. "And trying to keep that thing away from him. Now move before he figures out what we did."

We ran. The man rose but didn't come after us.

"Blackguards!" he shouted. "Thieves! Ruffians! You'll hang for this!"

The man didn't follow. There was no way he could

22

catch us, so we jogged to the dirt lane at the edge of the field and stopped near the farm.

"Maybe there's someone there who can help us," Mitch said.

I thought that was overly optimistic, and was about to say so, when the man began shouting again, alerting a woman who stepped out of a stone building behind the farmhouse, carrying a wooden bucket.

"Help! Ruffians," the man bellowed. "Thievery, assault! Help, help me, they're getting away."

"Uh oh," Mitch said. "We'd better move."

I ran as fast as I could, my head still spinning. "Where are we going?"

Mitch ran beside me, trying to bundle the cloak. "I don't know. I think this used to be the path that ran alongside the fields. If we're lucky, it will take us to the road that leads to Horsham."

We ran until the farmhouse was out of sight, and the sound of the man's shouting died away, then we stopped, gasping for breath, to take in our surroundings. Fields of green shoots bordered by rows of shrubs lined either side of the road. It appeared to be morning, as the sun was getting higher and the grass alongside the road glistened with dew.

Mitch rolled the cloak into a bundle to make it less obvious, the way Ellen had shown us the year before. "When do you think this is?" he asked.

"Don't know," I said, "but did you see the way that guy was dressed? It was a lot more modern than the last time we were here."

"But not very modern."

I shook my head and winced.

"You're bleeding," Mitch said.

I touched the side of my head. My hair was matted

23

and sticky.

"We need to get to Pendragon's house," Mitch said. "We need answers, and some help."

We hurried on, and soon came to a collection of houses.

"That can't be Horsham," Mitch said. "It's too small. It must be a new village."

There were few people out, and those we did see were too busy chopping wood or carrying water or tending horses to pay us any attention. We continued walking, keeping our eyes on the road and straining to maintain a normal pace so we didn't appear suspicious. When we came to a crossroad, we hesitated.

"If we are in the same place," Mitch said, "Horsham will be this way."

I looked up and down the road, which was rutted, muddy, and dotted with gaping holes. "It's sorta familiar, except it looks like no one's fixed it since last time we were here."

"Maybe we should ask, though," Mitch said. "If we're wrong, we could waste a lot of time."

I looked at the few men and woman in the village. "I suppose it won't hurt. It seems safe enough here."

Then I heard rhythmic thumping that grew louder and louder. I looked down the dirt track. A black horse galloped our way, urged on by the skinny man.

"Run," Mitch said.

"Thieves, ruffians!" The man's voice sounded above the pounding hooves. "Catch them."

We raced down the road as shouts erupted behind us. The hoof beats from the skinny man's horse grew louder.

"This way," Mitch said. We ran from the road into

a thicket, pushing our way through as branches and brambles slapped at our faces. We ploughed deeper into the wood, then entered a field. On the road behind us, the horse came to a stop.

"In there," a man said. "Let's get them."

"You go." It was the voice of the skinny man. "I'll get the mayor. He'll have more men. If they give you the slip, they'll catch them. Once the word goes out to the whole town, they'll never get away."

The sound of hoof beats faded as the horse galloped away. Behind us, the men shouted and cursed as they blundered through the bushes. We ran to the end of the field, then followed a dirt track away from the road and toward more farms and fields. We sprinted across open land, hid behind stone walls, in barns and under watering troughs, until we found a wide path that led to a line of trees in the distance, and a stone footbridge.

"That must be the river!" Mitch said.

We ran until our sides ached, then ducked behind a holly bush to catch our breath.

In a nearby farmyard, half a dozen men milled around, looking under wagons and searching the outbuildings. Silently, we left the cover of the bush and crept toward the river, keeping low. We hadn't gone far when we heard shouting behind us.

We raced for the bridge and, as we neared it, I glanced over my shoulder. "Five or six," I said, "but at least no one is on a horse."

Mitch nodded but didn't bother looking. "They're still going to catch us, though."

At last, we reached the narrow bridge and ran across, ducking behind the trees for cover.

I looked around. There were open fields, some

hedge rows, a stand of trees. "Where to now?"

Mitch pointed through the trees. "The river!"

The shouting and pounding of feet grew louder. "That's crazy."

"Exactly." He grabbed my arm and dragged me through the trees to the riverbank. We jumped.

The river was shallow, muddy and stinking of rot and manure. We slogged, waist deep in brown water, toward the bridge. With Mitch holding the cloak over his head, we squeezed into the narrow space where the bridge met the riverbank, just as our pursuers crossed.

The running stopped.

"Where are they?"

"Check the hedgerow."

"Search the bushes."

We held our breath and waited. Seconds ticked by. The men shouted and searched and soon the footsteps returned to the bridge and stopped.

"They could be anywhere, hiding in the field, lying low in a ditch."

"Mr. Farran isn't going to like this."

"Let him not like it then. We've done enough. If he wants them found, he can organize a search party and find them himself."

The footsteps retreated, back the way they had come. We waited. Silence. Then we climbed the bank and peeked cautiously over the bridge. The men were gone.

"Now what?" I asked.

"This river runs by Pendragon's house. If we follow it, at some point, we'll get there."

For a while, we slogged through the mud near the river's edge, hidden by the bank and bushes. When we felt we were far enough away, we climbed the bank and walked along a pathway. We passed fields, a few farmhouses and, occasionally, people, but they were always far away, or too preoccupied, to take notice of us. It also didn't hurt that we were covered in mud; it hid our odd-looking clothing and helped us blend in.

Soon, we came to another bridge, where the river widened and emptied into a long, narrow lake, with a pathway running along one side, and stone mills lining the other. The mills were busy, with men pushing carts, pulling horses, carrying sacks and shouting to one another, so we climbed onto the road, crossed the bridge and took the path. We were on the wrong side of the river, but the pathway was clear and the men on the opposite side seemed too busy to notice us. We were in full view, but none of them had paid us any attention. If the skinny man, Mr. Farran, had rallied the town to search for us, he had not yet enlisted their help, but I wondered how long it would be before he did.

We walked steadily, not hurrying, hoping to remain unnoticed, and when we reached the end of the mills—where the river returned to its natural, though wider, state—we jogged to the footbridge. It was in better shape than the last time we had seen it, and on the other side of the river there was a path that led back toward the mills. We followed it to where Pendragon's house used to be and found nothing but a bramble-covered mound.

Silently, we picked our way through the weeds, to the top of the mound. There, we scuffed at the earth with our sneakers until we cleared a small patch of dirt.

Mitch handed me the cloak and dug into the soil with his hands. Soon, he uncovered a large, squared off stone. "This has to be the place. That looks like part of the wall."

Then another voice, from the direction of the river, called out.

"Hey! What are you playing at?"

# Chapter 5

## Mitch

I froze and felt the blood drain from my face. A boy with broad shoulders and unruly red hair sticking from beneath a flat cap stood on the path. He wore a loose shirt, with the sleeves rolled up to his elbows, tucked carelessly into canvas pants, which were patched on one knee and held up with suspenders. He had his fists on his hips and a smirk on his face.

"Hey! You're the muck snipes old Farran was going on about. He's up on the High Street, bellowing about being ambushed and robbed. So, what are you doing here? Digging for treasure, or burying your takings?"

I turned to face the boy. "We're doing neither. And we are not thieves."

The boy cocked his head.

"Then what are you?"

"Travellers," Charlie said."

"And what's that you're holding?"

I held up the bundle. "It's something that belongs to us."

The boy's smirk turned to a smile. "It's a cloak. Farran said you were carrying a cloak. I didn't believe him. You really are a couple of daft dodgers, aren't you?"

I felt myself flush a second time. "Were you sent

to search for us?"

The boy shook his head. "No, I'm on my way to work, and I'm late already, thanks to Farran and his yammering. But here I am, and there you are, so give me one good reason why I shouldn't turn you in."

"Because we haven't done anything wrong," I said. "It was Farran who attacked us."

Charlie stepped forward. "I told you," he said, "we're just travellers—"

The boy's smile faded. "Don't sell me a dog. The truth, the real truth, and then I'll decide if you deserve to be handed over."

I sighed. "What do you want to know?"

"Start with your names," the boy said, "where did you come from, and where are you going?"

"My name is Mitch Wyman," I said, "and this is my brother, Charlie."

The boy's eyes went wide. Charlie leaned close. "This is where he calls us valiant knights from long ago," he whispered.

But the boy said nothing about knights. "Are you kin to the Wymans in Lancashire?"

"No," I said. "We're from Wynantskill."

He shook his head. "I know nothing of Wynantskill. What county is it in?"

That stumped me. "What does it matter?"

The boy hesitated. "Because I am John Wyman, from Hambleton, in Lancashire, and I know of no Wymans from Wynantskill. Is it in the north?"

"If you are a Wyman," Charlie said, "then this is the home of your ancestors. This pile of rubble was once the home of Pendragon, and his descendant, Aelric of Sussex. He is our ancestor, and it was he who journeyed to the north, where they called him

Aelric the Wanderer. His descendant was Baron Robert Wandermyn, from which the family name Wyman came."

Charlie stopped, looking pleased with himself. I was pleased too, certain it would impress.

But the boy, John, slapped his thigh and laughed. "You are daft. I had made up my mind to let you go if you admitted to being thieves and scoundrels, for at least then I would know you weren't liars, but your story ..." He laughed again.

Charlie waited for him to stop, then cleared his throat. "Well, are you going to turn us in? We told you the truth."

"Turn you in? I should," the boy said, then his face grew serious, "for you clearly are the vagabonds Farran is searching for, but you are equally not the ruffians he claims you to be. And your story, daft as it is ... I know of the Baron, and have heard legends of Aelric. How could you know them?"

"Perhaps," Mitch said, "we're related."

The boy rubbed his chin. "I should turn you in, if only for you own benefit. You are most certainly daft, and you possess a stolen cloak." Charlie began to protest. John held up his hand to silence him. "But you know my family legends. Therefore, you may be kin, and I can't put my kin in the cells, not without a fair hearing. And that is something you will not get from Farran."

"So, what should we do?" I asked.

"Get away from here as fast as you can," John said, as he turned and walked away. "Go to where no one knows you. And stay out of trouble."

"But we don't know where to go," I called after him.

"Or how to get there," Charlie said. "Can't you help us?"

"You really are daft," John said over his shoulder. "I'm going to get my ears boxed as it is. Sort yourselves out, you're not my problem."

Charlie sighed. "What happened to the awe-struck, 'You are the knights of old the legends spoke of'?"

We headed down the mound, back to the path, picking our way through the brambles. "Maybe he isn't the person we're supposed to meet?"

"Then who is?" Charlie asked.

"I don't know."

"Then what do we do now?"

"I don't know."

"Do you know anything?"

I scowled at him. "I know we're in big trouble. And I know I'm wet and cold."

I stuffed the cloak under one arm and  tried to put my free hand in my jean pocket, but it was too wet and clammy. So, I tucked it under my armpit instead. "We need to find somewhere to hide. Some place warm where we can dry out."

"Sure," Charlie said. "Any ideas?"

I sighed and said nothing.

Then, above the babble of the river and the distant murmur of men's voices came the sound of running. I looked and saw John racing toward us. We jumped aside to get out of his way, but he grabbed us each by an arm and pulled us after him.

I stumbled, trying to keep up. "What's going on?"

"This way," John said. "Quickly. If you value your lives."

He pulled us along until we could keep on our feet, then raced ahead, while we did our best to keep up with him. We crossed the foot bridge and headed into the church yard, dodging between the gravestones. In the distance, I heard men shouting.

"What's happening?" Charlie asked.

"News got to the mill," John said. "The men remembered seeing you on the path. Good job staying out of sight."

"Well, we're not exactly fugitives," Charlie said.

John kept running. "You are now," he said, not bothering to look back. "This way!"

We ran between houses and hedgerows, crossed a muddy street and raced around a small cottage. The land here was covered in tall grass. Not enough to give us cover, just enough to slow us down.

John didn't slow. "Come on."

At the end of the short meadow, we sprinted up a rise, crossed a muddy lane and slid down the opposite side. For a moment, we all laid in the grass, panting.

"What are you doing?" Charlie asked.

"I'm trying to save your lives," John said. "The millers are not interested in talking. They're looking to hang someone. Namely you."

"But you didn't care a minute ago."

John wiped sweat from his face and stood, listening. "I don't know if we're related, but I don't know that we're not, and I can't chance allowing my kinsmen to be hung on old Farran's say-so."

"So, what do we do?" I asked.

"Keep following me," John said, "and stay close."

He grabbed the cloak from me and started to run.

"Hey!" I called.

John kept running. "I'm not stealing it. I can run faster with it than you can. Come on!"

We raced after him, running in the gully next to

33

the lane, out of sight from anyone on the other side. After a while, the air began to smell of yeast, and we saw buildings ahead. John waved to us. "This way. There'll be people at the brewery. We don't want to be seen."

He cut around the brewery, using a hedgerow for cover, then ran to another road. When we caught up with him, he was crouching behind the bushes. "We're almost there, but we need to split up."

"Almost where?" Mitch asked.

John peered over the hedge and looked up and down the road. "My house. Well, my aunt Esther's house."

I didn't look, but I heard the clatter of horse carts and the sounds of people walking.

"No one seems to be looking for us," John said. "I'll go first. Charlie, you follow when you see me go up that side street. Then Mitch can start when you reach it. Walk. They are looking for two boys on the run. If you walk, you won't look suspicious, other than being soaked and muddy and dressed strangely."

He stood and walked into the road, holding our cloak under his arm as if he was on an errand. He crossed to the far side, walked past a few stores and houses, then turned down a side street. Charlie got up to go after him.

"Can we trust him?" he asked.

I shrugged. "To late to worry about that."

Charlie sighed and stepped into the road.

When Charlie got to the side street I stood up and followed, careful to keep a steady pace and not look at anyone. My face burned and my heart thumped so loud I was sure people could hear it. At the side street, I saw Charlie, a little way ahead of me, but there was no sign of John. After a few more steps, Charlie turned and walked up to a house. The door opened and he entered.

I kept my eyes on the door and concentrated on putting one foot in front of the other. I was sure I heard shouts and pounding feet behind me, but when I looked over my shoulder, there was no one there. It was just my mind playing tricks. I hurried to the house and knocked on the door. Inside, strident voices rang out. The door opened. I stepped in and found myself next to Charlie. "What's going on?"

"I guess Aunt Esther isn't as willing to help us as John is," he said, closing the door behind me.

From the next room, a shrill voice continued. "… and what do you think you're doing consorting with vagabonds, anyway? Is this how you repay my kindness?"

"I'm telling you," John said. "They aren't vagabonds, they're kin, Mitch and Charlie, brothers, from someplace called Wine-and-Kill. We owe them refuge."

"I don't care if they're the lost princes, they're still vagabonds, and we owe them nothing. Lord knows you bring in little enough to pay for your keep. Do you think your salary is going to cover the board of two wastrels looking to take advantage of a gullible young man?"

"You know," I said, running our family genealogy through my mind, "if his name is John and that's his aunt Esther, I think that makes John our great-great-great-great grandfather."

"Maybe we should tell Esther that," Charlie said." She might be easier on John then."

"Small chance of that," I said, looking toward the

doorway where the shouting was coming from.

Then John backed slowly into the room, trying to avoid a woman who continued to advance on him. The woman, with hair the colour of an old penny pulled into a tight bun, wore a drab dress, a damp apron, and a scowl. Attached to her apron by a pudgy fist was a young girl with strawberry blonde hair wearing a smock that dusted the floorboards around her feet. She had her fist pressed against her mouth and regarded me and Charlie with round eyes.

"I'm telling you, I think they're kin. They called themselves Wymans before I said who I was. They were at that mound, where you told me old Aelric lived. And they knew about our family."

"Kin my giddy aunt!" Esther said. "Anyone can go to that mound, and anyone can say anything they please. Who do you—"

Then she looked away from John and, for the first time, saw me and Charlie. She stopped in mid-sentence and looked back at John. "Brothers?"

John nodded.

"And they were at the mound?"

"I just told you—"

"And did they do or say anything?"

John shrugged. "Well, they were carrying this."

He unrolled the cloak, holding it up to its full height.

Esther reached out with a trembling hand, gave the cloak a tentative touch, then turned white, and crumpled to the floor.

# Chapter 6

## Charlie

"Mum, Mum!" the girl shouted. She knelt next to her mother shaking her, then turned to John. "Look what you've done! Get out. Take those boys with you."

John dropped the cloak and stood, dumbfounded.

"She's fainted," Mitch said, rushing to Esther's side. "Get her a drink of water. Help me roll her onto her back."

But the little girl began punching Mitch, and when I came to help, she started punching me too."

"Leave it, Maggie," John said. "Go get some water."

"No," she screamed. "I won't! Make them go. Make them go."

"Don't," Esther said. her voice barely a whisper. She moved her hand, resting it on Maggie's arm. "They must stay."

Maggie stopped screaming and grasped her mother's hand. "Mum, are you alright?"

Esther's eyes opened. She looked at me and Mitch, drew a halting breath, and her skin turned pale again.

"Breathe deep," I said. "Slow. Take it easy."

"You … it's not possible."

"What are you talking about?" John asked. "Do you know them?"

But Esther ignored him, and instead pulled her hand away from Maggie and stroked Mitch's cheek. "You're real."

"Of course they're real," John said. "What are you on about?"

Then she touched the side of my head, making me wince.

"You're hurt." She struggled to get up. We helped her to her feet, and she took my hand, pulling me toward the room she had come out of. "Come with me. I need to tend your wound. John, get them something to wear. We need to get them out of these wet clothes."

The room she led us into was steamy and warm, containing several washtubs, a huge stone sink and a wood stove throwing more heat than was comfortable. She sat me on a low stool and, after taking a wet rag from the sink, knelt next to me and began dabbing at the side of my head.

"Where am I supposed to get clothes from?" John asked. "I've only got these. I don't have any to lend them."

"Get some from the finished laundry, in the pantry."

"But you can't do that. You've got to deliver it today. If you're short—"

Esther continued cleaning my wound. "You let me worry about that, John. They must have clothes."

John left. Esther rinsed the rag, which had turned a pale shade of pink, in a nearby washtub, and went back to stroking my head.

"How did this happen?"

"A man saw us in his field," Mitch said.

I nodded. "Yeah, and he didn't want us there."

"He took the cloak from us."

"And when we tried to take it back, he hit me."

Esther leaned back and looked at me. "With what?"

I shrugged. "He called it a cosh."

"That's monstrous. Who would do such a thing?"

John returned, carrying a bundle of clothes. He dumped them at Mitch's feet. "It was old Farran. He was in town, trying to get a mob together so they can hang them. After a fair trial, of course."

"That man," Esther said, patting my hair with a dry cloth. "He will do no such thing." She ran her fingers over the side of my head. "You've got a lump, but the cut wasn't bad." Then she turned her attention to the pile of clothing, sorting through it and separating it into two piles: shirts, pants, suspenders. There was even a pair of socks and something that looked like underwear. "I'll need to apologize to Martha and make up some story for Louise. They'll need coats, and hats. Wait here."

She got up and left the room. John watched her go, shaking his head.

"I don't know what's gotten into her," he said. "First, she wants to throw you out, now she's putting her livelihood in danger. If we can't get these clothes to her customers by noon, she's going to lose business. Do you think, maybe that fainting made her soft in the head?"

"I don't think that's the case," Mitch said.

"Then why would she do this?"

"They're the knights," Maggie, staring wide-eyed at us, said.

John scowled at her. "What?"

"The knights, from the stories Mum tells me. Two

39

boys, brothers, with red hair, carrying a cloak, who come to visit. They're brave knights from an ancient kingdom, come to help us."

John made a noise that sounded like a cross between a snort and a laugh. "So far, it's us helping them. And they don't look much like knights to me." He kicked at the piles of clothing and grabbed Maggie by the hand. "Put these on." He tugged Maggie toward the door. "Let's leave these knights to it, Maggie."

Maggie allowed herself to be dragged away, but she kept staring at us until she disappeared into the next room. Me and Mitch took off our muddy clothes, rubbed ourselves down as best we could with them, and hurriedly put on our new ones before Aunt Esther came back. As it turned out, Maggie was the first to return. As soon as we had finished struggling into the unfamiliar garments, she peeked around the doorway.

"Are you really the knights?" she asked. "Did you save Aelric from the Normans? Did you help Pendragon—"

"Enough of that nonsense, Maggie," John said, stalking into the room. He gathered up our clothes and dumped them into one of the washtubs. "We've got enough problems without you weaving fantasies."

"I'm not," she said. "That's what Mum told me."

"Well, Aunt Esther's not daft enough to believe rubbish like that. And only a stupid girl could make up something so stupid."

Maggie scowled and looked at the floor as John walked past her. "Stay here. I'm going to see what's keeping Esther."

Maggie turned away from us, her shoulders

shaking. Then I saw a teardrop splash onto the floorboards. I went to her and put a hand on her shoulder.

"It's all right," I said, "he didn't mean it."

She sniffed and wiped her nose on her sleeve. "Yes, he did, and he says that you … that you're not …" She started sniffling again. I knelt next to her and turned her to face me. She continued to stare at the floor, so I hooked her chin with my finger and pulled her head up until she was looking directly at me.

"Don't be afraid to believe," I whispered.

Her eyes lit up. I put a finger to my lips, winked and went back to Mitch.

"What did you do that for?" he asked.

I didn't get the chance to answer. John and Esther returned, John carrying two pairs of old shoes, and Esther with two canvas jackets folded over her arm.

"These belonged to my Robert," Esther said, handing out the coats, one to me, one to Mitch. "You're big lads, I think they'll fit you."

Mitch's hung off him a little, and the cuffs fell to his knuckles, but mine fit fine. It was the opposite for the shoes. Mitch got a pair of low work boots that he said fit perfectly, while the leather shoes I wedged my feet into were so snug they pinched.

"They'll ease up after some use," Esther assured me when I told her. She looked us up and down. We were now dressed similarly to John, with rugged shirts, and pants held up with suspenders, though you couldn't see them now that we had jackets on.

"They'll need hats," Esther said, after finishing her inspection.

She left the room and returned a few seconds later holding two flat caps, like the one John wore.

"Will someone tell me what's going on?" John asked.

Esther placed a cap on Mitch's head. It was the same size as John's, but it came down to his ears.

"They're knights," Maggie said.

John scowled at her. "So you keep saying." He turned to Esther. "You were ready to throw them out, now you're treating them like royalty. And why is Maggie calling them knights?"

Esther placed a hand on John's shoulder and stared into his eyes. "John, listen. This is important. You wouldn't believe me if I told you the truth, so what I am going to say—what you must believe—is that they are ... cousins, of mine, from my father's side of the family. And they are here to do something important. And you have to help them."

"Why? What's so special about them?"

"They're knights," Maggie said.

Esther looked at Maggie. "They're cousins."

Maggie looked at me. "No, they're not. They told me—"

I winked at her. "We're travellers."

John glared at me. "From where?"

"A kingdom far away," Maggie said.

Esther sighed, looked at Maggie, then at me, and slapped the remaining cap on my head, pulling it roughly over my wound. "Wear these," she said. "They'll help you fit in. If you don't talk too much."

John shook his head. "This is getting ridiculous; I'm going to work before I get fired."

"No, John," Esther said. "You're staying here."

"What?"

"We need to help these young men."

"Why?"

42

"They're knights," Maggie said.

"We're travellers," Me and Mitch said together.

"Cousins," Esther said.

Then someone pounded on the door.

"Mrs. Marsden. I need to speak to you."

It was Mr. Farran.

# Chapter 7

## Mitch

We all fell silent and turned toward the door.

"Hide," Esther said. "Quickly. Quietly."

John headed out of the room, motioning for us to follow. In the main room, he climbed a narrow stairway. We followed, being careful to not make the risers creak. At the top of the stairs, the three of us crouched in the dim hallway to listen as Esther, with Maggie clinging to her apron, opened the door.

"Good morning, Mr. Farran," she said. "If you are here for May's rent, I'm afraid you're too early, I don't have it yet."

"Your nephew," Farran sputtered, "John, I need to speak to him."

"John left for work some time ago. Perhaps you should look there."

"He's not there, and these men saw him running away with the two scoundrels who tried to murder me this morning." A murmur of voices expressed agreement.

John stood, crept into the room in front of us and peeked through a small window. "There must be a dozen men out there," he whispered when he returned.

"Well, that's odd," Esther said. "I'm sure John would not consort with ruffians."

"Be that as it may," Farran said, "I still want a word with him."

"And I told you, he left for work some time ago."

The door creaked, then came a thump, as if someone slammed a hand against it.

"You won't mind if we search the premises, then?" Farran asked.

"Yes, I would," Esther said. "Now, if you'll excuse me, I have work to do."

"As your landlord, I can insist on entering the premises."

"And as a woman alone with a young daughter, I can insist that I do not want a dozen men in my home pawing through my belongings. It would be unseemly."

This time, the door slammed shut, and the bolt clicked into place.

"I will return with the law," Farran shouted. "And I'll not only search these premises, I'll have you evicted, as well."

The door banged again as someone—my guess was Farran—kicked it. Then silence returned.

John peeked out the window again. "They're leaving," he said triumphantly. Then he ducked. "One of them is staying. He's across the street, watching the house."

We rushed downstairs to find Esther with her back to the door, her face white. "You have to leave. Now."

"We can't," John said. "They'll see us. They left a lookout."

"Maggie," Esther said, pushing herself away from the door. "Gather their clothes, all of them. And the cloak. Put them in a laundry bag. John, you'll have to

45

go out the back door and circle round through the twitten."

"But the lookout—"

"Let me handle him."

Esther turned toward the kitchen as Maggie scurried in, hefting a large white sack that nearly outweighed her.

"Maggie, take that to Mrs. Hodges," Esther said, "ask her to hold it for me. But wait until I tell you."

John shrugged, looked at me and Charlie, and said, "I don't know what any of this is about, but come on. Let's go."

"No, John," Esther said. "Wait." She ran into the kitchen and returned a few moments later with a small clay jug. From inside the jug, she pulled a few notes and some coins. "Here," she said. "Take this."

John looked horrified. "Aunt Ester, I can't! That's your savings, the rent, how will you live?"

"Let me worry about that," she said, shoving the money into his hand. "You've got to get away and you've got to take Mitch and Charlie with you. Take a train, go to London, but get out of here before Mr. Farran comes back."

She turned to Maggie. "Let's go now. I'll see you out the door. Remember, Mrs. Hodges, tell her to hold it." She put a hand on the door latch, then looked over her shoulder at us. "What are you still doing here?"

"Come on," John said.

We followed him out the back door into a cluttered, dirt patch surrounded by a brick wall.

"Up here."

John hoisted himself onto the wall and jumped over. We followed.

On the other side of the wall was a narrow, brick-lined pathway. Charlie began jogging down it, away from the road.

"No," John hissed. "That's a dead end. We can only get out this way."

"But we'll be seen," I said.

John sighed. "We'll have to trust Esther," he said, then turned and sprinted quietly toward the road.

When we caught up with him, he was squatting by the weathered door that led to the street. He motioned for us to be silent and sit down next to him. From the street outside, I heard a door open.

"Be quick now, Maggie," Esther said. "There's more work to do."

"Hey," came a voice from across the street, "What are you playing at?"

"My business," Esther said. "My daughter does deliveries for me. You're welcomed to look in the bag. I assure you, my nephew is not in it."

"Mrs. Marsden," the man said, "Mr. Farran just wants a word with him. You've nothing to worry about."

"And I told Mr. Farran that John is not here. But he has insinuated I am lying and is going to set the law on me. I think I have plenty to worry about, don't you, Mr. O'Connor?"

"I, well, perhaps it is getting out of hand."

"Would you like to search my home? Perhaps that will convince Mr. Farran."

"But, wouldn't that be unseemly?"

"My daughter is on an errand, and I will wait out here on the street. I would rather have you go through my home than Mr. Farran and his mob."

"I don't know. I don't think Mr. Farran—"

"Please, I want to put this matter to an end. I have work to do, and so do you."

"Well, I suppose it can't hurt," the man said, his voice drawing nearer.

"Thank you," Esther said. "I'll stay out here until you are satisfied John isn't hiding inside. I am trusting you to be discreet with my belongings."

"Certainly, Mrs. Marsden."

A door closed. Quick footsteps on the pavement. The door we were crouching behind swung open.

"Quickly," Esther said.

Charlie turned down the street, in the direction they had come from.

"No, you daft dodger," John whispered, "You want to run right into Farran and his gang? This way."

We followed John down the street, running as silently as we could. He led us down another alleyway that emptied onto a large grassy area. There, we were hidden among bushes and low trees, dodging from one hiding place to another until we saw a low, brick building.

John pointed. "That's the train station." But he didn't lead us to it. Instead, we worked our way around it, continuing away from the town, until we came to a railroad track.

"Why didn't we just go to the station," Charlie asked, as we sat down on the grassy rise near the tracks.

"Sure," John said. "We'll just waltz into the station and ask for three tickets to London. That won't draw any attention at all." He shook his head, looking at the ground. "No wonder Esther wants me to take care of you."

"Well, if we're not buying a ticket, what are we

going to do?" I asked.

"The train won't pick up speed until it passes through the town," John said. "And at this point, it will be coming slow out of the station."

Charlie's eyes widened. "You mean we're going to jump on it?"

John smirked. "What, you've never hopped a train before?"

# Chapter 8

## Charlie

"Of course not!" Mitch sputtered. "How could we? Why would we?"

Then came the sound of a shrill whistle, and the growl and hiss of a steam engine.

"Well, you've got a reason now," John said, creeping up the bank. "Come on."

I rolled my eyes and mouthed, "He's crazy," to Mitch, then followed John.

We laid in the low grass near the top of the rise, listening to the chugging of the train as it grew louder and nearer.

"The trick," John said, raising his voice to be heard over the engine, "is to not let the train crew see you. Stay hidden until I move, but follow quickly. We only get one chance at this."

I glanced down the track as billowing smoke and a screaming black engine came closer.

"Anything else we need to know?" I asked.

"Yes." John said, as the train reached us and the engine thundered passed, "Don't fall."

A coal car clattered passed, then a passenger car, then another. As the third one approached, John jumped up and ran. Mitch followed. I jumped up, slipped on the gravel and fell. As I scrambled to my feet, I saw John jump onto a step in front of one of the doors and cling to a hand-rail on the side of the carriage. I raced forward, watching as Mitch, running for all he was worth, reached out his hand. John grabbed him and pulled him up. I was glad for that, but realized I was still far away. I ran faster, but the train, although travelling slow, started overtaking me. John and Mitch called and waved, but they moved farther and farther away.

Then John pointed toward the train. I looked. Another carriage, and another doorway, was coming my way. With my heart pounding and my feet slipping, I grabbed the handrail as it sped by and clung to it as the train dragged me along. With a final push, I reached the step and crouched there, hugging the handrail and panting until the smoke and ash from the engine sent me into a coughing fit.

The train rumbled by brick buildings, stone store houses and rows of brick homes. Then I saw Mitch and John flatten themselves against the door to the carriage they were clinging to, and John motioning for me to do the same. I stood on the step and pulled myself close to the door, wondering why, until we came to the bridge. The gap between the iron railing and train carriage was a matter of inches. I sucked in my stomach and held my breath until we crossed.

Once we hit open land, the train picked up speed. I clung to the handrail, my knuckles white, as trees, houses, farms and fields whizzed by. Then the door bumped, the window slid down and a voice yelled, "Hey! What do you think you're playing at?"

I looked up. A man with a moustache, blue uniform and a conductor's cap was glaring at me. Then a brawny hand shot through the window and grabbed me by the throat. "C'm 'ere, you little

51

scallywag."

The conductor slammed me against the door and, for a moment, I feared he was going to pull me through the tiny window, But then the door swung open and the conductor's other hand grabbed me by the arm. I clung to the door, watching Mitch watch me, his eyes wide with fright. John wasn't looking my way. He had pulled their window down and was reaching through it. That's all I saw before the conductor yanked me into the carriage.

He grabbed my collar with both hands, slammed me against the wall, and shoved his face against mine. "Nobody gets a free ride on my train," he shouted. His breath stank of stale tobacco, making me gag. I gulped in some air. "Sorry."

The conductor slammed me against the wall again. "Sorry? You're not sorry yet."

He let go with one hand and I watched him draw it back and curl it into a fist. I ducked my head as far as I could and put my hands up, waiting for the blow. Then I heard a shout.

"Don't hit him, Mister, we have money. We can pay."

I dropped my hands and saw Mitch and John running down the carriage, between rows of seats crammed with people. The passengers seemed to be divided into two groups: those who tried to ignore what was happening, and those who gaped at us with undisguised glee. The latter group was the larger by far.

The conductor looked at John. "Money, eh?"

"Yes, sir," John said.

Then the conductor grabbed him with his free hand and slammed him up against the wall next to me. "And where did the likes of you get all this money?" He glanced at Mitch, who was backing away. "You're the murderous little ruffians who tried to do Mr. Farran."

"We never—"

The conductor pinned both me and John to the wall with one arm and made a swipe at Mitch with the other.

"Break!" I gasped.

"Damn right I'll break you," the conductor roared.

Mitch looked at me, then at the conductor. "How?"

"I'll show you how," the conductor said, raising his fist.

Then John kicked him in the knee.

The conductor howled. John squirmed away, Mitch dropped to the floor while John stomped on the conductor's foot, which made him loosen his grip on me. I pushed forward, making him step back, and fall over Mitch.

"Help! Murderers! Thieves! Stop—"

I jumped forward, landing on the conductor's chest with both knees. A whoosh of air came out, and he lay still, gasping, his eyes wide and angry. Some of the passengers screamed, others shouted, and a few jumped from their seats and came toward us.

"Run!" John said.

We pushed through the door at the end of the carriage and raced across the rickety connecting bridge to the next car. Our pursuers were already tumbling through the door when we jumped into the next carriage and ran down the aisle. As they entered the carriage, the men chasing us shouted. "Thieves! Stop them!"

Several of the men in the carriage jumped from their seats and ran toward us.

John turned. "Run!"

We ran back up the aisle, toward the other men still streaming into the carriage. John stopped. Looked behind us, looked in front of us, and then at the carriage door.

He ran to it, threw it open and, with a shout of, "Follow me," leapt out.

# Chapter 9

## Mitch

I couldn't believe what I'd just seen. I looked at Charlie, then at the men closing in on us.

"Go!" Charlie shouted. Then he ran to the door and disappeared. If he screamed, the roar of the engine and the shouting of the men swallowed it.

I took a breath and ran to the door as men from behind and in front made a grab for me. A smoky wind hit me as I leapt from the train. Then I was sailing through the air, and then I was being poked, scratched, punched and generally beaten up by the bushes and weeds alongside the track. I tumbled and bounced over broken stalks, briers and stones until I at last came to rest in a patch of weeds.

I tested my limbs, but none felt broken, just bruised. Then I crawled to the clear area at the edge of the track to look for Charlie and John.

The train was long gone. I could still hear it in the distance, and smell the smoke, but there was no sign of the men who were after us. They seemed very eager to get their hands on us in the train, but none of them, it appeared, were so eager that they followed us out the door. I took that as a good sign.

A ways down the track, Charlie and John were heading toward me. John was limping and brushing leaves from his clothes, and Charlie was bleeding from a scratch on his cheek. John was carrying a flat cap, even though he and Charlie were still wearing theirs. I reached up to feel my head and found mine was gone.

As Charlie and John drew near, and I saw how dishevelled they looked, I began to feel I had gotten off lightly.

"Are you okay?" I called to them.

Charlie gave me a weak wave. "I think so."

"You're bleeding," I said, as he came closer.

He put a hand to his cheek then looked at the blood on his fingers. "Just a scratch. My landing wasn't as soft as yours."

Then John put the flat cap he was carrying on my head. "Next time you jump from a train, remember to hold onto your hat."

"There won't be a next time," I told him.

He smiled, then looked behind me, at the patch of weeds I had come to rest in. His smile disappeared. "Uh-oh," he said.

"What do you mean, uh-oh. I'm fine."

Then I felt a tingling in my hands. Seconds later, it turned into a painful itch that spread to my arms, my face, my neck, and then I was on the ground, writhing and scratching and screaming.

# Chapter 10

## Charlie

I saw it before Mitch felt it: red welts appearing on his hands, face and neck. Then, seconds later, he was on the ground.

"Quick," John said, rushing by me.

"Where are you going," I said. "We've got to help Mitch."

"We are," John shouted, not turning. "This way!"

I ran after him and caught up as he began pulling broad leaves from a patch of weeds. He stuffed some into my hands and grabbed up some more. "Let's go."

We ran back to Mitch, still screaming and thrashing. John crushed the leaves and rubbed them on the bumps. "Help me," he said.

I started doing the same, crushing the leaves by rubbing them between my hands, then smearing them anywhere I could see a rash. Slowly, Mitch stopped thrashing, and we rubbed more on him. His screams turned to moans and, finally, he just lay there, panting.

"What … what happened?" Mitch asked.

"You landed in stinging nettles," John said. "We rubbed some dock leaves on you, that should to the trick."

"It hurts, and itches like crazy."

"Yeah," John said. "The dock leaves will take the edge off it. You'll be fine in a couple of hours."

"Hours?"

We waited until Mitch was ready to move, then we started walking down the track, away from Horsham and toward Three Bridges, John limping, me bleeding, and Mitch covered in green goo and red welts.

John walked next to me for a while, silent, then he asked, "What did you do to that conductor back there on the train?"

"Knocked the wind out of him," I said. "It gives you time to get away, while they try to catch their breath."

John looked down at the tracks. "Don't ever do that again."

"What?" I sputtered. "Why? We've been doing it since we were kids."

"Well, you're not a kid anymore," John said. "Jumping on someone like that, you could seriously hurt them, or even kill them. We're in enough trouble as it is."

I felt my face go red. "Sorry."

"Don't be sorry," he said. "Just don't do it."

I stared down at the track, feeling foolish, and a little ashamed, but John put a hand on my shoulder. "Don't worry. No harm done. And there are better ways to incapacitate someone."

"Really? How?"

"Someday, maybe I'll show you." Then he pointed to the side of the track. "Look here, a stream."

We left the track and gratefully washed in the cool water. Mitch was especially glad because the water soothed his skin and washed off the green slime, but then the itching came back. John said we could hunt

58

up some more dock leaves, but Mitch said he'd tough it out.

We kept walking. Fields, hedgerows and trees stretched out on either side of the tracks, so there was no need for caution. When we approached a small station—Faygate, John called it—we left the track and circled around it, through the fields. We weren't afraid of being spotted and identified, but we didn't want anyone there telling Farran they had seen three boys wandering through. After we left Faygate behind, we heard the rumble of a train coming our way, so we left the tracks to stand in the weeds (after checking for stinging nettles) and watched it go by.

"That'd be the train to Horsham," John told us. "It'll load up there and return to Three Bridges, and it'll get there a lot sooner than we will."

We walked on. None of us asked what we were going to do once we got to Three Bridges, because none of us knew. All we did know was that we couldn't go back to Horsham and, since Three Bridges wasn't Horsham, that was our only option.

We crossed a trestle bridge over a large pond and approached a curve in the track that John told us led to the nearby village of Crawley. "Another half hour or so," John said.

Then I saw a group of men walking on the track, coming toward us. I thought they might be railroad workers, or just people travelling, like us. But one of them wore a conductor's uniform, and the others looked like policemen. Then one of them pointed at us and shouted. "There they are!"

# Chapter 11

## Mitch

There were six of them, and they were coming fast.

"Run," John shouted.

We ran back along the track as fast as we could without tripping on the ties. I looked over my shoulder. They were gaining on us. "They came looking for us," I said. "How did they know we were here."

"The conductor must have spotted us when the train went by," John said.

"If the conductor saw us," I said between gasps, "and he was on his way to Horsham, how did they find out?"

"You never heard of a telegraph?"

"Of course I have, but I didn't know you had them yet."

"Less talk," Charlie said, already breathing hard, "more running."

We pushed harder. The bridge was ahead of us. It looked like we might make it, but we wouldn't get much further, they were gaining fast, shouting and waving sticks that looked like a longer version of Farran's cosh.

"Any ideas?" John asked.

"No," Charlie said. "Other than a miracle."

Then we heard a whistle in the distance.

"I think we might have got one," John said. "Faster. We need to get across the bridge."

We doubled our efforts. My legs felt like jelly and my lungs burned, but I pumped my legs as hard as I could, struggling to keep up with John.

We got to the bridge, and down the long, straight stretch of track I saw a train coming at us.

"We can't be on the bridge if a train is coming," I shouted.

"I know," John said. "So run faster."

We raced across the broad expanse, my lungs burning and my heart a lump of ice slipping into my stomach. The train was closing in on us, and the men were catching up with us, and the far side of the bridge still looked a long way away.

"We're not … going … to make it," Charlie gasped.

"Yes, we will," John said. "The train slows down here, because of the curve."

It was madness, running toward a moving train, even if it was starting to slow down, like John said. The only good thing about it was the men behind us seemed to be smarter than we were. They fell behind, two of them not even rushing onto the bridge, and the other four now in the middle, while we were almost at the far end. But so was the train.

The whistle screamed, the brakes shrieked, smoke, sparks and steam billowed, and we ran headlong into it.

"Jump," John shouted.

We leapt from the track and dropped about ten feet, landing in the weeds and rushes growing in the boggy ground near the water's edge.

61

Behind us came a splash and I looked to see the men who had been following us, sputtering and flailing in the middle of the pond.

"C'mon," John said, pulling himself from the mud, "this way."

Charlie and I dragged ourselves through the weeds and saw John rushing up the embankment toward the train. "This way," he shouted. "Hurry!"

We climbed up as quick as we could and stood next to him, huffing and panting, as the train chugged slowly onto the bridge. John watched as the last carriage rolled by. "Get ready," he said.

"For what?" Charlie asked. But John didn't answer. He just shouted, "Now!" and bolted toward the train, and we stumbled after him.

John caught up with the train and pulled himself onto the small platform at the end of the final carriage. I ran after him, and he pulled me up. I leaned against the carriage, gripping the door handle, gasping for breath. John turned to help Charlie up, but when I looked, I saw Charlie was falling behind.

# Chapter 12

## Charlie

I saw the train pulling away and tried to push harder, but my legs refused to go any faster. I felt ready to collapse on the tracks and die from exhaustion, then I heard Mitch and John shouting. I looked up. They waved their arms and pointed. I took a glance over my shoulder and saw one of the men coming toward me. He was wet and muddy and must have climbed onto the bridge as the train went by, and now he was chasing me back across it.

Panic spurred me on. I ran faster than I thought I could, and the train came nearer. But so did the sound of running footsteps from behind me. I was close to the train, but not close enough and, even though it was going slow, it began to pull away from me again.

Mitch shouted to John, "Hold onto me," and pulled his jacket off. With John holding him, he leaned as far forward as he could and, gripping one sleeve, threw the coat toward me. "Take this."

I grabbed for the coat, but it slipped away. He threw it again and the sleeve barely reached me. He leaned further and threw it again. I grabbed the end of the sleeve and Mitch and John slowly drew me in. Holding the coat meant I could keep up with the train, but my feet couldn't run that fast. I fell forward, throwing my other hand out to clench the coat. John saw what was happening and braced himself and Mitch gripped the sleeve tight, twisting it around his fist.

I was so close that I didn't fall flat on the track. Only my legs, from the knees down, hit the cross ties, but they took a pummelling.

"Hold on," Mitch shouted, whether to John or me or both of us I couldn't be sure. I was sure, however, that he wasn't trying to encourage the man behind me who, when he saw me fall, dove forward and grabbed me around the knees.

Mitch gritted his teeth and groaned, pulling me closer while John struggled to keep his feet, and Mitch, on the platform. The man hugging my knees was being dragged along the tracks. He shouted and cursed and clawed his way toward my waist.

"Pull me in!" I shouted.

Mitch reached out. "Hold on!"

I grabbed his hand.

Mitch pulled me an inch closer. "The rail, grab the rail!"

"I can't." The man gripped the back of my shirt and began pulling himself forward. "He's pulling me down."

John braced himself and wrenched Mitch to the side. I swerved with him, and the man holding me—at the end of the human chain—swung wide, hitting the rail. Then John wrenched Mitch back the other way. The man skidded across the track and bumped over the opposite rail. With a scream, he lost his grip on me and tumbled over the side. Then next thing I heard was him splashing in the water.

"Don't drop me," I screamed.

"Bring him in, bring him in!" John shouted, pulling Mitch upright. I grabbed the rail and together they hauled me onto the platform where the three of us collapsed into a panting, gasping heap.

# Chapter 13

## Mitch

We jumped off the train before it got to Crawley station so we wouldn't be spotted catching a ride again.

Because we knew they were looking for us at Three Bridges, John said we'd need to walk further up the line to Horley. We took the roads from Crawley to Three Bridges and then up to Horley, fairly certain that no one but the railroad police would be looking for us.

On the roads, we made better time, and in another hour we entered Horley station, dusty, tired and hungry.

Even though we were in Horley, John thought it best for us to split up while we were at the station. "I'll get my ticket first," he said. "Then wait for a bit, let a few people go ahead of you, then buy yours."

"How do I do that?" I asked.

John looked exasperated. "You go to the counter and ask the man for a third-class ticket to London."

He stuffed some coins into my hand. I looked at them, and then at John. "But how much is it? What should I give him?"

John sighed. "Haven't you ever gone on a train before?"

Both Charlie and I shook our heads.

"Do you still ride horses where you come from?"

"We don't have horses," Charlie said. "We have cars and buses and—"

"No, we haven't ridden on a train before," I said, interrupting Charlie. "Not inside, at least."

So, John explained in detail what to do and what to say and how the money worked, and we watched from a distance to see what he did and then waited a while.

Charlie bought his ticket without incident and walked onto the platform as he had seen John do. I leaned up against the brick wall and waited, counting as five people entered the station, then I went inside.

"Third-class ticket to London, please," I said to the man behind the counter. He was dressed in a uniform, like the conductor, and the man we had recently dumped into the pond, and I felt fear rising in my chest.

The man looked at me and the money in my outstretched hand, but instead of taking it, his brow furrowed, and he asked. "Why are you going to London?"

The question took me by surprise. "I, well, I'm—"

"It's just you're the third young man in the past half hour that's bought a ticket to London. You going to see the Exhibition?"

"I … yes," I said, "yes that's it."

The man smiled. "It'll be a sight. Even though it doesn't open for a week, there'll be a lot to see."

I nodded. "I'm sure there will be."

The man reached for my money. "We've been warned about a gang of ruffians. You wouldn't know anything about that, would you?"

"No," I said. "No, sir, I don't."

The man smiled and handed me my ticket. "No, I suppose you wouldn't. You don't look like a ruffian."

I took my ticket. "Thank you," I said, and started for the platform.

"You be watchful in London, son," the man called after me. "Bad sorts of people up there. And steer clear of ruffians."

"Train's due in five minutes," John said, when I joined him and Charlie on the platform.

"They know about us," I said. "The railroad guy said they were warned about a gang of ruffians."

"We need to stay split up then," John said. "Third-class will be at the end of the train."

He turned and walked away, and Charlie, without even glancing my way, ambled in another direction. I looked down at the platform and wandered away from them, walking nearly the whole length of the platform before I heard the train approaching.

The engine slid by, growling and belching smoke. I walked quickly toward the rear car and as I passed the first-class carriage I turned and froze. Farran was in the carriage, staring out the window at me. Then a cloud of smoke obscured my view and when it cleared, I saw it wasn't Farran at all. The seat was empty.

I hurried on, trying to keep my imagination from panicking me again. Ahead of me, John and Charlie entered the third-class carriage. I followed them on and wedged myself into a seat. We remained separated and didn't speak to each other. This wasn't hard because the carriage soon filled up and made moving or talking almost impossible. With a lurch, the train pulled away from the station and I felt a weight lift from my shoulders.

We stopped at several stations where even more people jammed into the car, making for a hot, noisy and smelly journey. And long. It seemed to take forever, but that was probably because it was so uncomfortable, and I was still nervous about Farran and wouldn't feel totally safe from him until we could melt into the crowds of London. As the train pulled into yet another station, I glimpsed through the tiny bit of window I could see between the crammed bodies and saw we were in a place called Norwood Junction. There were, I heard people around me saying, only a few more stops to go.

I sighed, feeling relieved, but then, when the train remained still, I felt my fear rising. The people in the carriage began to grumble. John looked my way and inclined his head toward the door, then he motioned to Charlie and the three of us muscled our way toward the exit.

"What's going on," Charlie whispered as we elbowed our way through the crowd.

"I don't know," John said, "but I don't like this."

"But if we get off—"

"If the coast is clear, we'll take the next one."

We made the door. John reached for the handle, but the door snapped open before he could touch it. Outside the open door stood Farran and three police officers.

Farran pointed a gloved finger at us. "That's them."

# Chapter 14

## Charlie

Rough hands grabbed my throat and dragged me through the train door onto the platform, along with John and Mitch. None of us had time to react or even shout.

"Well, gentlemen," Farran said, turning away from the policemen and grinning malevolently at us, "I trust you can hold these ruffians, until such time as they can be returned to Horsham for trial."

The policeman gripping my throat grinned just as maliciously at me. "Oh, don't you worry, sir. You can count on us."

"For your sakes, I hope so," Farran said. "Now if you'll excuse me." He turned and strolled down the platform, calling out to a conductor as he passed by, "Get this train moving as soon as I board. I have appointments to keep."

The conductor removed his hat and ducked his head. "Yes, sir."

Farran stepped into the first-class carriage. The door slammed, the engine shrieked, and the train pulled away, leaving me, Mitch and John struggling for breath while the three policemen held us by the throats, our feet barely touching the platform.

That was all I saw because the police then dragged us off the platform, through the station and onto the street, shouting at us the whole way and giving us the occasional cuff across the face. The shouting appeared to be for the benefit of the public, who gaped at the brave policemen subduing a trio of boys. The slaps to the face, however, seemed to be just for the joy of it.

The only good thing was, we weren't taken far. The police station was near the railroad station and once we were dragged through the door, they stopped hitting us and threw us on the floor, instead.

The station was dark and cluttered and cramped. A wooden desk and chair took up the space along one wall, and above it a chalk board displayed a messy grid filled in with illegible names. I had no time to register anything, other than the grey-haired policeman sitting in the chair, before a heavy boot struck my side. I groaned and curled into a ball and felt hands going through my pockets.

"What's this?" one of them asked.

"Looks like a glass cutter," another said.

"You steal this?" The question was punctuated by another kick. "You using this as a weapon?"

Then I heard John yell, "Hey! That's mine! Give it back!"

The sound of a boot striking flesh caused him to stop.

"Lying thieves."

The sound of another kick, this one to Mitch, whose groan I recognized.

"Another glass cutter?"

"This one only has money. They managed to steal a tidy sum."

I heard the clicking of coins and looked up to see the policemen dividing up the money.

71

"Hey! That's my mon—"

John was cut short by another kick to the ribs. The policemen pocketed what was left of Esther's money and threw our glass cutters into one of the desk drawers.

"Lock them up, Isaac," one of the policemen said. "They're wanted for robbery, assault and attempted murder. We're holding them until Horsham sends someone up to collect them. In the meantime, we'll go see if we can return this money to its rightful owner."

The three of them laughed, and Isaac said, "Oh, aye," in a way that made me believe they had decided that the rightful owner was the bartender at the nearest pub.

Isaac might have been the oldest of the group, but he was still strong. He grabbed me by the back of the neck, dragged me down a short hallway and threw me into a room. I tried to stand but was too sore. Then Mitch landed next to me, and a few seconds later John landed on top of us.

"Get comfortable," Isaac said, "you're going to be here a while." The door clanged shut, footsteps retreated to the office, the chair creaked under Isaac's weight and silence returned.

John moaned and rolled onto the stone floor.

"Attempted murder?" Mitch asked.

Slowly, John stood. "Yes, old Farran is going to credit us with every crime he can think of. He won't rest until we swing."

I rolled over and rubbed a hand over my aching ribs. "What are we going to do?"

John flexed his arms and legs and, clutching his sides, drew a deep breath. "Anything broken on you?"

Mitch patted his sides and his legs. "No."

"What are we going to do?" I asked again, trying to stand.

"We're going to get out of here," John said. "Quick. Before the others come back."

"What?" Mitch asked.

"How—"

But John cut me off. "No time. Just lay there and pretend to be hurt. And when Isaac comes in, block the door to keep him from leaving."

"We're not going to lock you in here with him," Mitch said.

"No! Just block the door," John said. "I want him to go for you."

"What—?"

"Now lay down and look hurt," John said, already moving toward the door.

I laid on the cold stone. "That won't be hard."

John pounded on the door. "Hey! Hey, you thieving bastard!" he shouted through the iron grate. "Want to know where I got that money from?"

"What I want is for you to shut up!" Isaac shouted from the other room.

"I was pimping your wife! But it took me all day to get that little bit because she was too ugly to charge the going rate."

Footsteps pounded down the hall before John had even stopped talking. He jumped back from the door. "Get ready!" he hissed.

Isaac slammed his palms against the door. "Shut your gob-hole you little piece of shite, or I'll give you what for."

"Strange," John said, "that's what my customers said while they were having your wife."

The door slammed open, just missing my head. Isaac bellowed and charged at John, who ducked out of the way as Isaac swung at him.

"C'mon," I said to Mitch. We jumped up as fast as we could and stood in front of the door.

Isaac saw us in an instant. "Oh, pulling that old trick, eh?"

He reached for us and grabbed us each by the throat. Then John was on him, his arms wrapped around his chest, squeezing hard. Isaac let go of us and tried to shake John off, but he kept his arms locked, squeezing harder. Then Isaac went red, and he slumped to the floor.

"What just happened?" Mitch asked, as John searched Isaac's pockets.

"Did you kill him?" I asked.

John yanked coins from one of Isaac's pockets and stuffed them in his own. "No, he's just unconscious. Hurry, we've only got a few seconds."

Isaac moaned and made a feeble grabbing motion with his hand, as if he thought he still had his hands around our throats. John leapt over him, and we rushed out of the cell, slamming and locking the door behind us. Isaac was already shouting and banging by the time we got to the door.

"Our glass cutters," Mitch said. He ran to the desk and yanked the drawer out. It must have been where they stored bits of evidence, because screw drivers, knives, a cosh, and our cutters scattered over the floor.

"No time," John said. "Let's go."

Mitch scooped the cutters from the pile of weapons. John pulled the door open.

The three policemen were walking up the steps.

# Chapter 15

## Mitch

I stuffed the cutters in my pocket and raced toward the door, just in time to see the policemen outside. They were as surprised to see us as we were of them, and for a moment, no one moved. Then John slammed the door and threw the bolt.

"C'mon!"

Banging and shouting from outside the door joined Isaac's shouts and bangs as we raced around the small room in a panic.

"What do we do?" I said, raising my voice to be heard above the din.

John pointed. "The window!"

Above the desk was a small window, covered by a metal screen. The screen was hinged and held in place by a sturdy padlock.

"We can't break through that," Mitch said.

"There has to be a key for it," John said, already pulling out the other desk drawers. Papers, Ink bottles, pens, pencils, old fashioned handcuffs and a bottle of whiskey spilled across the floor. John and I pawed through it, looking for keys.

"Up there," Charlie said, pointing to a board on the wall with several sets of keys hanging from it.

John grabbed them. With a sweep of his arm, he cleared the top of the desk, jumped up and began trying the keys.

The shouting at the door stopped and the thumping became louder and more rhythmic.

"I think they found a battering ram," I said, watching the door bow and strain with each boom.

"Hurry," Charlie said.

The lock snapped open. John threw the screen up and the door splintered.

"Go!" John shouted.

He dove through the window. Charlie scrambled onto the desk and squirmed out after him. The policemen clambered over the remains of the door as I jump up on the desk and crawled through. Charlie and John grabbed my hands and someone else grabbed my foot. I held tight to Charlie and John.

"They've got me."

"They're out the window," one of the policemen shouted. "Go round the back."

"They're coming," I said.

John and Charlie pulled. I kicked with my free foot, hit something soft, and the hand holding my leg let go. I flew out the window and the three of us landed in a heap amid the scruffy weeds, rubble and broken glass of the alley.

"Go, go go!"

John was already up and running. We ran after him.

We raced down the alley, cut through a narrow gap between two buildings, crossed a street, and ran down another alley. After zigzagging through back-streets and alleys, we came to the railroad tracks. Then we ran down the path next to the line until we were in the countryside. Even then, we kept running. When we came to a brick archway under the tracks with a stream running through it, John stopped.

"In here," he said.

It was a big arch. We only had to duck a little as we sloshed through the water. When we were halfway through, John leaned up against the damp wall. "This will do."

I rubbed my hands together against the chill. "You're kidding."

"They'll see us in here," Charlie said.

"Not if we flatten up against the walls," John said. "They'd need to come into the tunnel to see us, and I don't think they're that keen. Besides, I think we lost them in town. They're probably still searching the ginnels around the station, if they've not already gone back to the pub."

"So, how long do we stay here," Charlie asked, holding his hands under his arms.

"Until it gets dark," John said.

Charlie gaped at him. "That'll be hours."

"Get comfy, then."

We leaned against the moist stones, our feet braced against the other side of the tunnel to keep them out of the water as much as possible. And we waited.

"That thing you did," Charlie said after a long silence, "with Isaac. Was that the thing you were telling me about?"

"Yeah," John said. "If you squeeze hard enough, you can make people pass out. It works better if the person takes a few deep breaths and holds it. We used to do it to each other for laughs when we were kids." He looked at Charlie. "And it doesn't hurt, and it won't kill you."

Charlie nodded.

"What are you talking about?" I asked.

"John has a better way to incapacitate someone," Charlie said. "He doesn't want me jumping on anyone."

"We're in enough trouble as it is without you killing someone."

"I wasn't going to kill anyone, and I—"

"We're in enough trouble as it is," I said, "without us arguing."

John and Charlie descended into sullen silence.

And we waited.

# Chapter 16

## Charlie

I knew John was right, but it bugged me that he was being so smug about it. And I was cold, and tired, and hungry, and thirsty, and standing in freezing, foul water that I wouldn't have drunk even if I was dying.

I guess John was getting fed up too, because it was still light when he led us out of the tunnel.

"It's not night," he agreed, "but it is late in the day. And don't worry about the peelers, they'll be measuring the pavements upside down by now."

Mitch stared at him. "What?"

"Drunk, you know," John said, "jiggered, ossified, in their cups, with the money I got from Aunt Esther."

That thought seemed to depress him, so we just kept walking, not even asking where we were going.

We walked north, as the daylight slowly faded, through village streets and towns, over roads that were alternately paved and smooth, or muddy and pock marked.

We didn't talk much. John told us a little about his life in Lancashire, and we told him nothing, which didn't seem to bother him. And we didn't mention that we'd passed this way before, once marching around the city to meet Harold's army, and again with Ellen, on our way into London to seek our fortune.

Neither trip had ended well, and I didn't hold out much hope for this one, either.

We did manage to get some food and drink using a portion of the money John had left. He was reluctant to part with it, but we were all—including him—starving and dying of thirst, so when we saw a street vendor in one of the larger towns, John bought a loaf of bread and a bottle of beer from him, carefully dropping a few of his coins into the vendor's outstretched hand. The bread was stale, and the beer tasted foul, but we were all grateful for it.

"There's only a little left," John lamented as we ate our meagre meal. "I've got to pay Aunt Esther back. She'll be ruined, thrown out on the street, with Maggie."

We tried to reassure him but, doubtful that things would turn out all right ourselves, we weren't very successful.

As night approached, the villages and towns grew larger, more crowded, and closer together. And the larger they got, the worse they smelled and the more dilapidated the buildings became. Then it started to look vaguely familiar.

"We're in su'thuk," I said to Mitch.

Mitch looked around, then nodded.

"You know London?" John asked.

"Well, sort of," Mitch said.

John narrowed his eyes but said nothing.

As we went deeper into Southwark, the lanes became more crowded. Then the stench of the streets was cut by the stench of the river, and we got our first view of London, with the glow of light illuminating parts of the city.

"My god," I said. "They've got electric lights."

"Electra-what?" John asked.

"Lights," I said. "They aren't using torches anymore."

"You mean the gas light?"

I shrugged. "Yeah, I guess."

"Look over there," Mitch said, pointing down-river. "That's the Tower. And that must be London Bridge ahead of us."

I gazed at the bridge. It was mostly shrouded in darkness, but I could tell it didn't look anything like London Bridge. "Where are all the houses?"

"They took that bridge down twenty years ago," John said. "Are you telling me you've seen it?"

"Well," I said. "In photos, and stuff."

"Photos?"

"He means drawings," Mitch said.

There were no houses or markets or shops or street performers to slow us down, so crossing the new London Bridge didn't take long. I also noticed there were no heads on pikes being displayed at the Southwark entrance to the bridge. I sort of missed the clutter and confusion of the performers, but I didn't miss the heads.

When we got into the city proper, we stopped on a crowded street corner, trying to stay out of the way. Then we wandered into an area with no lights, only the occasional torch, where avoiding pedestrians became a challenge, so we headed back to an area with streetlights. The gaslights weren't as bright as electric lights, but they were better than torches. I could even read the road sign.

"We're on Bishopsgate Street," I said. "We've been here before."

John looked at me in surprise. "I thought you

said—"

"We need to find someplace to hole up for the night," Mitch cut in.

John put a hand in his pocket and pulled out his few remaining coins. "There's not enough money left for lodging."

"Then we'll have to find a doorway or an alley to sleep in," I said.

John scowled. "That will be dangerous."

"Or we could just walk around all night," Mitch said.

"All right, all right" John said. "But let's see if we can find someplace more secluded." He stuffed his hands in his pockets and led us in the direction of the river. "This was a bad idea. Why did we come to London in the first place?"

"Because no one knows us here," I said.

Then I bumped into someone tall and muscular and wearing a dark uniform that, in the gloomy half-light, was all but invisible. I bounced off him and nearly fell. "Excuse me," I said, then added in the hopes of avoiding a scene, "My fault."

The man looked at the three of us, and we looked back. His uniform had shiny buttons down the front. He wore a tall hat, had a truncheon in his belt and a surprised expression on his face.

"It's you," he said. Then he pulled a strange wooden device from his pocket and began spinning it around, making a loud rattling sound. "The Horsham Gang, the Horsham Gang," he shouted, grabbing me by the arm.

"Run," John yelled.

"No," Mitch said. "He's got Charlie."

"Thieves, murderers," the cop shouted. But he

wasn't shouting at us, he kept spinning the rattle and seemed to be calling out to the street.

"C'mon," Mitch said, grabbing my free arm. He yanked me toward him, trying to break the cop's grip, then John joined him but all they succeeded in doing was make me the rope in a tug-o-war.

The cop dropped his rattle and reached for his truncheon.

"No," I shouted to Mitch. "Break!"

Mitch let go and dodged away. The cop raised his truncheon but was put off balance by Mitch suddenly letting go. He teetered a bit, and I tried to pull John forward as Mitch slammed into the back of the cop's knees. We tumbled into a heap. The truncheon clattered to the cobbles, and we jumped up and ran.

"Stop them!" the cop shouted. "They're thieves and murderers."

The rattle started up again and then we heard it echo from the nearby lanes.

"He's calling reinforcements," John said.

We raced through the streets, pushing people out of the way, dodging down narrow lanes. Behind us, the sound of feet slapping on the cobble stones grew louder as more people joined the chase. I didn't bother to turn around to see if they were cops or just people joining in the fun; there wasn't time, and it didn't matter. If anyone got their hands on us, we were done for.

We ducked down a dark side street, but that didn't slow our pursuers down. As we dodged around a corner we hesitated a moment, trying to decide which way to go.

"Over here," a voice called.

We looked around. The shouting and tramping of

feet grew closer. Then a wooden panel opened on the wall of a run-down building, and a skinny boy in ragged clothes beckoned us. "This way! Hurry!"

I looked at Mitch, Mitch looked at John, John looked at me and we all shrugged and clambered through the hole. The panel banged shut behind us as, just beyond it, we heard our pursuers trample by. The four of us sat in the dark, holding our breath—or at least trying not to wheeze too loudly—and waiting. Outside the shouts of anger turned to confusion. The crowd split up, searching the alleyways and side streets and eventually they moved far enough away for us to relax.

"Thanks," I said. "I think we're safe now."

I started to push on the panel, but a hand landed on my shoulder. Then I heard a door bang, and the flicker of a torch lit the tunnel. The boy, silhouetted by the glow, crooked his finger at me. "This way."

"Thanks," John said. "But we're not—"

The torch came closer, and a thin man with straggly hair, wearing clothes only a little less tattered than the boy's, appeared out of the gloom. He squatted and gave us a gap-toothed smile.

"I believe," he said, pointing into the darkness behind him, "that the boy said, 'This way.'"

# Chapter 17

## Mitch

John stood and took a step back. "I don't know."

"Really," Charlie said. "I think it's safe enough now. We'll just go."

"And not partake of our hospitality?" the man asked. "We just saved you. The least you can do is join us for some conversation."

John took another step back. "We'd rather—"

The man stood. "I insist."

Shadows moved behind him. Several boys, big ones.

The man looked at John. "We can offer you a safe bed, food and drink."

I could practically feel John wavering. It was a tempting offer—too good to be true—and we didn't have the option of refusing.

I knew what they were, and what they were going to pull us into if we couldn't get away. But there seemed no way to back out. Then I had an idea.

"Thank you," I said, hoping I sounded sincere, "especially for the safe bed. Those cops aren't going to stop looking for us. We'll gladly come with you. Is your place well-fortified, and armed?"

"Armed?" one of the shadowy boys from behind him asked.

"Yeah, we killed one of them," I said. "They'll

85

have the whole force out after us."

"You did a peeler?"

"Sure," Charlie said, picking up the tale. "We broke out of their Podunk jail and one of them got in our way. So, we snuffed him."

The man looked like he didn't believe us, but his gang were taking the bait.

"Jail?" one of the boys said.

"Broke out?"

"Snuffed a peeler?"

"That's right," I said. "And when they find us, they won't be taking any prisoners. Not us, or anyone helping us."

The boy who had opened the panel went to stand next to the man, no longer eager to be near us. The man handed him the torch. "You're soft, the lot of you. Murder? I think not. Help me take them, lads."

He came at us, his hands reaching out. There was no room for our usual ploy, and the boys behind him, although not advancing, didn't look as intimidated as they had been. I nudged John and stepped forward. "Show him," I said as the man came for us.

John leapt forward, grabbed the man around his chest, and squeezed. I stepped back to the panel and nodded to Charlie. We each put a hand on it, ready to push. Seconds later, John stepped away from the man and let him slump to the floor.

"He killed him!"

We didn't wait to see if they were frightened or emboldened. Charlie and I pushed the panel. The wood snapped and clattered to the cobbled street. We jumped out, followed by John, and no one else.

We weren't being pursued, so we didn't run, but we did walk fast, away from the gang, avoiding the lit streets, and being careful to keep away from people. It was dark and silent, but occasionally—as we wandered through the maze of narrow lanes and alley ways—we heard laughter, or music, or voices raised in anger coming from the dilapidated buildings. We had no idea where we were heading, but we kept moving in the direction we hoped would take us toward the centre of the city.

Half an hour later we were hopelessly lost, and on the edge of the gas-lit streets.

"We'd better backtrack," John said. "We'll be easily seen in the light."

Charlie pointed. "What's that?"

I looked. In the distance, dim in the dark, was a massive dome with a spire on top.

"It looks like the US Capitol building," Charlie said.

John shook his head. "It's St. Paul's Cathedral. At least now I have half a notion where we are."

"Should we go there?" I asked.

John shrugged. "It's as good, or bad, a place as any. Just be careful."

We tried to keep to the shadows, but most of the streets were lit by gas-lamps. We crossed a wide thoroughfare, dodged a band of late-night revellers, and hid in an alley when we saw two policemen strolling along the sidewalk. Then, at last, we came to the church.

It was enormous, and lit with a few gas lamps that made it look sinister in the gloom. But it was quiet there, and peaceful and we sat on a wall outside the church doors, feeling safe for the first time since our arrival.

"It sure doesn't look like it did last time," Charlie

said.

I nodded but said nothing. Sitting still after being chased and pummelled and held captive was nice, but it allowed the chill to seep into me. John was uncomfortable too. He got up and stood in front of us, hugging himself and shifting his weight from one foot to the other.

"We should have gone with them," he said. "I know they didn't mean to treat us well, but we'd have been safe, warm, and fed. And we could have stolen some blankets from them when we escaped in the morning."

Again, I said nothing. He was probably right.

"We should keep moving," Charlie said. "It's cold sitting here."

"And where are we going to go?" John asked, a hard edge to his voice.

I sighed. "I don't know."

"You must have a plan."

"Wait for morning," I said. "Then see what happens."

He hung his head, gazing at the pavement. "That's not much of a plan. Don't you know what you're here for? Aunt Esther thinks you're something special. Surely you have a plan."

"It's complicated," I said.

"There's always a plan," Charlie said, "but we don't always know what it is."

"So why are you here? What's this all about? Who are you, anyway?"

I cleared my throat. "It's—"

"Complicated," John said. "Yeah, I got that."

No one said anything for a while, then John raised his head. "When are you from?"

"Don't you mean, where?" I asked.

John shook his head, staring up at the church. "No. That's not important." He took several deep breaths. "Aunt Esther, she thinks you're knights, from ancient times, and that's crazy. But she made me go with you, and now we've been chased, incarcerated, and we're all three headed for the gallows. I didn't ask for this, but I'm as involved as you two. I may as well be hung for a sheep as a lamb, so tell me whatever it is you know. I think I deserve an explanation."

I sat silent for a few moments, thinking. "Well, we're not knights," I said. "I don't know why Esther thinks that."

"That I can believe. But you talk like you've been here before, so you're either incredibly old, or you're from some …" He trailed off, not daring to think what we couldn't bring ourselves to say.

"It's hard to believe it ourselves," I said. "And to speak it out loud, you would think—"

"You're crazy, yeah, I know," John said. "But Aunt Esther is willing to ruin her life for you, and I've risked mine, repeatedly, for you, and nothing you say is going to sound crazier than you being knights."

"You're right," I said. "We're not from the past. We're from the future."

Silence. Then John asked, "How far?"

"The year two thousand and seventeen," I said. "When we left, it was Saturday, the eighth of July."

More silence. "That's one hundred and sixty-six years from now," John said.

"So, this is eighteen fifty-one?" Charlie asked.

John looked startled. "You don't know?"

"We never know," I said. "We just … go. We're

wanderers, like your kinsman, Aelric, who we did meet. We go where we are sent, but we never know when it's going to be."

"Or what we're going to do when we get there," Charlie added.

"So why do you go?"

I looked at Charlie. "I guess, because we know we're meant to."

"But you don't know what you're meant to do?"

"No," I said, turning back to John. "We have no idea why this is happening to us."

"But you must have some idea. What have you done before? How does it work?"

"We always have something that we bring with us," I said, "and that usually has a significance."

"And we usually meet up with an old Druid," Charlie said, "who helps us."

"And we always encounter a magic stone called the Talisman," I added, figuring it couldn't sound any crazier. "And—"

"Hold on," John said. "You always bring something with you, something of significance. What did you bring this time?"

I pulled the glass cutter from my pocket. "This."

John looked at the cutter and smiled. "Then I know where you're meant to be—the Exhibition."

I jumped off the wall and stood next to him. "The Exhibition?"

"Yes," John said, excitement in his eyes. "It's made of glass. They call it the Crystal Palace." He pointed at the glass cutter. "Can you use those things?"

"Well, … sorta," I said.

"I can," Charlie said, holding his up.

"Then you could get jobs there."

I shook my head. "They might not want us."

"Well, yeah, maybe," John said, "but, the Crystal Palace, and you have glass cutters. You must be meant to go there."

"The guy I bought the ticket from asked if I was going," I said. "He seemed to think I should."

"You were told about the Crystal Palace, and you didn't think to tell us?" John said.

"I didn't have a chance, did I?" I also hadn't had the chance to tell them about suspecting Farran was on the train, but I thought it best not to reveal that.

"But you were told about it," John said. "And you have glass cutters." He paused. "And you don't have any other plan?"

Both Charlie and I shook our heads.

"Then let's go. It's not far, and the walk will warm us up."

We followed him away from the church and back to the streets. "Where are we going?" I asked.

John kept walking. "To Hyde Park."

◆

We had been to London before, but John knew it better than we did. He led us to a wide lane called Fleet Street, then onto The Strand, which he said would lead us in the right direction. Along the way, he asked more about our adventures, and how the cloak worked, and I tried to give short answers that wouldn't make us sound crazy.

"You have to be asleep for the cloak to work?" he asked, as we emerged from an alley, having dodged yet another group of drunken men. "Why is that?"

I shrugged. "We don't know."

91

"And you always come to Horsham? What's so special about Horsham?"

I shrugged again. "We don't know."

"And that Druid bloke, if you always meet him, where is he?"

"We don't know."

"And your magic stone, the Talisman, where is that?"

"We don't know."

John shook his head. "For people from the future, you don't know very much."

"Being from the future doesn't make us geniuses," I said. "In fact, we always feel pretty stupid in the past. Everything is so different, it's like we don't know anything."

John smirked. "I grant you that."

"Cop," Charlie said.

We scuttled into an alley and waited until the policeman passed by.

"We're near the Royal palace," John said, "there'll be a lot of cops and guards around. We'll need to be careful."

"How do you know that?" I asked.

John looked at me. "Are you telling me you don't know where the Royal Palace is?"

"Of course we don't. We're Americans. Do you know where the White House is?"

"The White what?"

"Exactly."

John shrugged. "Well, I do know that, just ahead of us, is Trafalgar Square, and beyond that is Pall Mall, and then the Queen's Palace. If we head north, we should find Oxford Street, and that should lead to Hyde Park."

We couldn't think of a better plan, so when the street was clear, John led us off the Strand and back into the darker lanes, where we zigged and zagged and eventually came to Oxford Street.

For being 'not far' away, we did a lot of walking. And the need to constantly hide and sneak through back streets meant it was some time before we came to the park. It was immense, and guarded by fences, rows of trees and, we were certain, security men— either the men guarding the Exhibition Hall, or the Queen, or both. We slipped in and made our way across the broad, grassy plains.

"It's huge," Charlie said. "I feel like we're in the country."

"I think that's the idea," John said. "To let the city-folk know what the rest of the country looks like. Or what the Royals believe it looks like; I've never seen farmland so neatly trimmed. Come on, let's go find the Exhibition."

Once inside the park, however, John became confused, confessing he didn't actually know where the Crystal Palace was.

"I thought you told us it was in Hyde Park," I said. "We're in Hyde Park, so what's the problem?"

"Well, it's big," John said. "I thought we'd get to the park, and it would just, you know, be there."

We wandered along paths, through ornate gardens, past fountains and down tree-lined lanes until we came to a proper road. In the grey light of early morning, we saw that the road led over a long lake, and on the other side of the lake was a huge, dark shape rising high into the air.

"That must be it," John said.

As we got close, the structure loomed larger, and

turned into a construction zone, and soon we were surrounded by stacks of lumber, piles of bricks and row upon row of large crates—many of them two or three times as tall as us—covered in canvas.

"We're on the site," John said, sounding surprised, awed and a little bit worried. "There will be guards here, security men. We need to hide."

We inched forward, sneaking from one canvas-covered crate to another, watching for guards, until we found a crate that had been unpacked. One side was lying on the ground under mounds of straw and the canvas was lying in a heap next to it. We laid down inside the crate, on the straw, pulled the canvas over us and, with the sounds of the city coming to life around us, fell promptly to sleep.

# Chapter 18

## Charlie

The sun was rising when the canvas was ripped away and I felt a boot in my side. The second morning in a row I was awakened this way.

"Hell-o, what's this?" a voice said.

Another boot in the side. I groaned, and then Mitch and John did too.

"Be off!" the voice shouted.

"Off my arse," another voice called. "Get Morgan. He can hold them until we turn them over to the Bobbies. Little blighters are surely here thieving."

John jumped to his feet. "We are not thieves."

A big man, wearing a dirty shirt, black vest, and a flat cap, pushed him back down. "Says you."

"We're not some street urchins, we've got money." He pulled the coins from his pocket to show the man. "We just didn't have enough for lodging."

"If you were looking for lodgings," the man said, "what are you doing here?"

By now, other workers were gathering around, eager to see what was happening and blocking the opening of the crate.

"Thieving, for sure," another man said. "Likely stole that money."

"We are not thieves," I shouted. "What is wrong with you people?"

The man reached forward and grabbed me by the shirt, pulling me close. "Don't you talk to me like that, you little cur. I'll teach you how to address your betters."

"What's going on here?"

I collapsed onto the straw as the man let me go. Everyone else took a few steps back, then a man with thick, grey hair and mutton-chop sideburns stepped to the front of the growing mob. The man who had threatened me with lessons about talking to my betters removed his hat. "Nothing, Mr. Paxton, sir," he said. "We just discovered these boys hiding in this crate."

The man, Paxton, turned toward us. "Explain yourselves." He didn't seem angry, simply impatient.

John snatched the cap from his head, and we did the same. "We're from the country," he said. "We, me and my cousins, we came here looking for work."

The men looking on burst into laughter. A look from Paxton silenced them.

"Then I fear you have wasted your time," Paxton said. "There is no work here. Not for you."

Then a stocky man wearing a blue coat, derby hat, and a look of officiousness, elbowed his way through the crowd and stood next to Paxton. "The police have told me to be on the lookout for a band of boys, wanted for robbery and murder," he said to Paxton, while glaring at us. "These could be them."

"We're not murderers," Mitch sputtered.

"Or thieves," John said.

"We will let the local constabulary decide that," Paxton said. "Then he turned to the man in the blue coat. "Mr. Morgan, I will leave them in your charge." Then he looked around at the other men, as if

96

surprised to see them all. "What are you all gaping at? There is work to be done."

The crowd dispersed, Paxton turned away and Morgan came toward us. "Don't even think about running away," he said, as if reading my mind. "There's a hundred men on this site for each one of you and they'll all be on you before you take ten paces. Now come with me, you lying rat-bags."

"The boys are not lying." We looked beyond Morgan and saw an old man carrying a broom walk up to Paxton.

"What of it, Mr. Merwyn," Paxton said. "We've no place here for them."

"This is my business," Morgan snarled at Merwyn. "Keep out of it."

Merwyn ignored him. "When the exhibition opens," he said to Paxton, "I will need boys like these to keep the underside of your exhibition hall from filling up with the detritus that falls through the floors. And in the meantime, there is still much work to do."

Paxton grunted. "I won't have them on my payroll, and I haven't time—"

"I'm certain they will work in exchange for a place to sleep and a bite to eat. I know them, they are hard-working, loyal, and honest."

Paxton looked at us, scowling, then back to Merwyn. "You can vouch for them?"

Merwyn nodded. "I can, and I do."

"Then it's on your head," Paxton said, already walking away. "Mr. Morgan, leave them."

Morgan turned toward us, his face red with rage. "I'll be watching you," he growled, then followed after Paxton.

Merwyn walked toward us. He was dressed in a loose, cotton shirt with pants held up by suspenders. On his head was the seemingly obligatory flat cap, He had thick, grey hair, a bushy beard and moustache, and piercing blue eyes. On his face, a scar ran up his right cheek and around his eye, ending in the middle of his shaggy eyebrow. "Mitch, Charlie," he said. "I am pleased to see you again." Then he turned to John. "And nice to meet you."

"Mendel?" I asked.

"It's Mr. Merwyn, now."

John gazed at him, open-mouthed. "Is this your Druid?"

Everything stopped after that because, as we walked out of the crate to greet Mendel—I mean, Mr. Merwyn—the Crystal Palace came suddenly into view.

How do you describe something that is indescribable, something that the world has never seen before, and will never see again, especially as it first appeared to me, with the rising sun hitting the panes of glass, making the palace glow like fire?

My breath caught in my throat. Mitch and John stood beside me, and I could tell they were feeling the same. It was, to use a wholly inadequate word, big. Not big like St. Paul's Cathedral—you could fit four of them into the structure I was now looking at—but big like the state plaza in Albany, if the plaza was a hundred feet tall and made of glass.

The palace was tiered, like a wedding cake, with a slightly smaller section sitting on top of the huge base structure, and another, slightly smaller section sitting on top of that. In the centre was a grand entrance, fronting all three stories, with a domed roof on top. And yet, for all its size, it wasn't heavy and foreboding, like the stodgy structures of the Albany Plaza, or even the grim magnificence of St. Paul's. It was, instead, a palace of light, in every sense of the word.

It was constructed, from end to end and top to bottom, of symmetrical iron arches filled with glass panels. Even the roof, including the domed centrepiece, was made of glass. The iron arches were surprisingly thin, leaving the largest area possible for the glass, but they must have been stronger than they looked, for they held up the entire structure.

People and horses were everywhere, hauling crates, sawing wood, and clambering about on the iron frame. Flags flew from poles, landscapers planted bushes, men pushed wheelbarrows in every direction, and it seemed a city in and of itself, while London disappeared into the background.

"Impressive, isn't it," Mr. Merwyn said after a while.

John's mouth was still hanging open. "It's … I … we …"

"Come along," Mr. Merwyn said, "Let's go inside. There's work to be done. And much to learn."

We followed him around the crates and through a door, craning our necks the whole time.

"Watch where you're going," Mr. Merwyn told us. "You don't want to trip over anything."

Inside, it looked like a great exhibition hall, which, I suppose, is what it was. Spaces for exhibits—from booths to entire rooms—lined the hallways, both on the ground floor and the gallery above. Many of them were filled and being tended to by people I assumed to be the exhibitors. The place was so big and open there were actual trees inside. And not trees they

99

planted, but trees that had already been growing in the park. The central area had a huge tree in it that reached nearly to the domed roof, but it was still dwarfed by the size of the space, which also contained a stage and rows of tiered seating, in preparation for the opening ceremonies that were happening in just under a week.

We told Mr. Merwyn about our adventure so far, and introduced him to John, who still couldn't think of anything to say, and we continued through the main hall before entering a service area through a cleverly concealed door. From there, Mr. Merwyn brought us to some rooms and told us that this was where we would stay while we were working at the Exhibition. They were storerooms, cluttered with brushes, rags, brooms, rope, canvas and other odds and ends. Most people would think it a crime to make someone sleep in a place like that, but we were thrilled simply to have a safe place to go.

I wasn't thrilled, however, when Mr.Merwyn handed me a broom.

"But what about these," I said, taking the glass cutter from my pocket.

"The glass work finished here weeks ago," Mr. Merwyn said. "Mr. Paxton kept on a few of the glaziers for repair works so, despite all this glass, there is no call for your services."

Mitch took out his own cutter and held it up, running his thumb over the cutting wheel. "Then why do we have them?"

Mr. Merwyn smiled. "That, my young friends, is a mystery for you to solve."

Then he put us to work, but not before breakfast, which was the first real meal we'd had since our arrival. There was a portable restaurant, of sorts, on the site and Mr. Merwyn brought us there. John took out his meagre amount of money but Mr. Merwyn told him the canteen, as he called it, was free for the workmen, so we ate our fill, even though we weren't actually workmen.

The rest of the morning was spent sweeping the immense halls, cleaning out the exhibition stalls, helping unload crates and staying out of Mr. Morgan's way. As head of site security, I assumed he was a busy man, but he seemed to have time to pop up unexpectedly in the areas we were working, always glaring at us as if we had just pinched something. Or perhaps he was just angry that we hadn't, because it meant he couldn't take us into custody and hand us over to the police.

Throughout the day, Mr. Merwyn took us to different parts of the hall, taking us through the narrow corridors behind the exhibition stalls and showing us the world that existed beneath it, where we would be working when the exhibition opened. It was just high enough for us to crawl on our hands and knees, but it covered the entire area of the hall, which would have made it a vast, unbroken space if the floor above our heads hadn't needed to be held up with countless support columns. Still, it wasn't too cramped to work in, but we expected it would be less pleasant after people started dropping all manner of stuff through the floor.

At first, I thought the gaps between the boards were to conserve wood and keep down costs, but Mr. Merwyn explained that Mr. Paxton had designed it that way, so the floor the public walked on would stay clean. Dust, dirt and anything else that was dropped on the floor would be swept through the cracks by the long dresses of the ladies. The gaps also allowed cool air to be drawn up from below, as the warmer air escaped through hinged vents in the roof. It was an ingenious set-up, but I couldn't imagine what it would be like down below once the crowds arrived.

In the afternoon, Mr. Morgan stopped popping up around every corner. I guess he figured we weren't going to steal anything, or at least that he wasn't going to catch us at it. Mr. Merwyn then led us to another part of the hall, where some exhibits from the Monarchy were on display. It was a strange exhibit— consisting mostly of artifacts and other bric-à-brac of historical interest—and not in keeping with the rest of the exhibits, which focused on advancements in technology. Although how a penknife with 1,851 blades, or a mechanical talking head were considered technological advancements, I couldn't say.

But then we came to the final stall, a closet-sized room enclosed in glass and protected by a wooden railing to keep the crowds at a distance. Inside there was a single pedestal, and on top of the pedestal, propped up on a small, velvet cushion, was a black disc.

Both me and Mitch were stunned into silence, but John leaned over the rail, trying to get a better look at the curious object. "What is that thing?"

"That's the Talisman," I whispered to him.

"Really? I was expecting something a bit more grand," he said. Then he looked at the information plaque. "And what does it say here? 'This obsidian stone was once believed to contain magic powers. It is two or three thousand years old, originating in the Neolithic age, and is thought to have entered into the

Royal Collection during the reign of Queen Elizabeth.'"

I looked at Mr. Merwyn, who was gazing at the stone with a melancholy look on his face.

"This is what it has come to," he said.

"At least it's safe," Mitch said.

Mr. Merwyn nodded. "But no more than a trinket. These people, who now believe they control the Land, put their faith in machines. They ignore the true power, and therefore, it cannot help them. And it cannot help the Land."

John leaned over and whispered in my ear. "I see what you mean about him being a Druid. He is a bit mystical."

Mr. Merwyn looked at him. "It is no mystery. The Talisman protects the Land, but only if the Land protects the Talisman. With no belief, there is no protection. This foolishness is leading mankind to a dangerous place."

John looked up, past the gallery above us, to the glass ceiling and the iron framework. "Whoever built this wasn't so foolish."

Mr. Merwyn followed his gaze, then looked to the left, and to the right. "You find this grand?"

John nodded but looked a little uncertain. "I do."

"For that, I cannot fault you," Mr. Merwyn said, "for Mr. Paxton, the architect of this building, is a clever man. And Albert, the Queen's husband, has a grand vision. But their enthusiasm is misplaced. This glass and iron structure is a cathedral to the works of man, an altar where they worship themselves. But that path leads to darkness, a deep darkness that makes me fear for the Land. The only hope we have is if the Talisman is returned to the Sacred Tor."

I looked at the Talisman. "How are we going to do that?"

"You have the cloak?" Mr. Merwyn asked.

"Yeah, sort of," I said. "It's with John's Aunt Esther."

Mr. Merwyn nodded. "That is sufficient. It can be retrieved once we have the Talisman."

"So, we're going to steal it?" John asked.

Mr. Merwyn shook his head. "No. It belongs to the Monarchy, having been entrusted to them over two centuries ago. It must be returned willingly, so you—the Guardians—possess it by right."

"And how is that supposed to happen," Mitch asked. "They're not exactly going to hand it to us."

Mr. Merwyn smiled and shook his head. "Almost certainly not. But this is why you are here, to find a way to possess the Talisman, and to return it to the Tor before it is too late."

I looked at the Talisman. It really would be easy to steal it, I mean, to take it. It was secured, but a wooden rail and a glass case wouldn't protect it very well and, besides, we had access to the back entrances of the stalls. It would be so easy to take it. Having it given to us was another matter. I was about to ask Mr. Merwyn if he had any sort of plan in mind when we heard people approaching. One voice was that of Morgan, and the other belonged to Farran.

# Chapter 19

## Mitch

"Farran," I said. "What's he doing here?"

"I don't know," John said, "but we can't let him see us."

"This way," Mr. Merwyn said.

He led us to a nearby, unprotected exhibit, featuring a dummy dressed in an underwater diving suit, the kind with a helmet and a porthole. We hid behind a wall where we couldn't be seen, holding our breath.

Then we heard Farran's voice. "Most impressive. It is an amazing collection. Nearly as amazing as the building it resides in."

"Yes," Morgan said, "the whole package is like something the world has never seen. It will keep them quite mesmerized."

Their footsteps drew closer. We tried to shrink into the wall, but then they stopped.

"And what is this?" Farran asked.

"A trinket," Morgan said. "Some ancient relic of the Royals."

There was silence for a while, and I imagined Farran peering into the Talisman. Then he said, "Fascinating. Is it really that old? Would it be too much to ask if I could hold it?"

Morgan hesitated. "It would be possible, yes, but

we must be discreet."

"Of course."

Keys jingled. A panel slid open. Then silence.

"Mr. Farran," Morgan asked, "are you quite all right."

More silence.

"Mr. Farran."

"It's … sorry. Mr. Morgan, when you held this stone, did you see anything reflected in it?"

"Simply my own face. Now let me take this back. It needs to be returned to the display case."

"Oh, yes, certainly, certainly. Here you are."

"Are you sure you're all right, Mr. Farran?"

"It's nothing. I think I'm simply overcome by all this grandeur. Perhaps a bit of refreshment is in order."

"An excellent idea, Mr. Farran."

Footsteps. We tensed. But they were going away from us, and then I heard Farran's voice as if faded down the corridor. "The exhibits, are any of them for sale …"

We came out of the exhibit, back into the corridor.

"What was that about?" John asked.

"Farran touched the Talisman," I said. "He saw something in it. That makes him dangerous."

"He was already dangerous," John said.

"Well, now he's doubly so."

"Old Farran's got more clout than I thought," John said, "to be able to talk Morgan into giving him an unofficial tour."

"I think they might be friends," Charlie said.

"Could be," John said, "they did appear chummy. But now that the tour is over, he probably won't be back."

"Well, I'm not taking any chances," I said.

Charlie nodded. "He touched the Talisman. He will be back."

"Charlie is right," Mr. Merwyn said. "If the Talisman has shown his black heart that his fondest desire is going to come true, he will not be able to resist returning to it. We must keep watch. And you must stay out of Mr. Farran's sight."

There wasn't any arguing with that, so we left Mr. Merwyn and went back to work, taking care to keep to the back corridors and service areas.

We worked through the afternoon, ate at the canteen, then worked into the night. At length, however, all the men went home, except for the night watchmen. Soon, the grounds became deserted, and the great hall fell into a deep, eerie silence.

We went back to the storeroom Mr. Merwyn had shown us in the morning, hoping to find him there, but the room was deserted. No one seemed to know we were there, we had no idea what to do and no idea where to go so, since it was dark and we were tired, we rolled up in blankets and fell asleep on the floor.

◆

"What have we here?" a voice said, pulling me from sleep. "A trio of stowaways."

I expected a kick in the ribs, which had become my morning alarm clock lately, but the remark was followed instead by a soft chuckle, and I realized it was Mr. Merwyn.

"It is very convenient, you sleeping in here," he continued. "You would be in deep trouble if discovered, but I think the risk is worth the

107

advantage. Take care that no one spots you; my influence carries only so far."

We went to the wash house, then to the canteen, and then to work. Mr. Morgan harangued us more than usual in the early hours and appeared to be in a foul mood.

"I think he had a tussle with John Barleycorn last night," John said, "and John Barleycorn won."

Charlie looked at him, confused. "What?"

"He's hung over," I said.

We speculated about Morgan and Farran and their possible connection, and whether Morgan's condition might be related to the refreshments Farran had suggested, and whether Farran would be back and if he really would try to steal the Talisman and what we could do to prevent that, but then Morgan appeared and growled, "less talk and more work," so we kept our thoughts to ourselves after that.

We spent the morning outside, raking loose straw into piles and loading empty crates onto wagons. After lunch, we swept the great hall, and managed to manoeuvre ourselves to the section set aside for the United States. In addition to a huge eagle statue and cluster of flags, there were exhibits featuring dental appliances, a double grand piano, and a display of pistols and rifles. They looked like early revolvers, and some of the rifles also had cylinders, turning them into six-shooters. We were interested because they were so old, and yet brand new, while John was strangely impressed that they could fire six shots. When he saw we weren't as awed as he was, he asked how many shots rifles could fire where we came from. I was going to try to explain machine guns to him, but then I thought, if he was so overwhelmed by a six-shooter, the idea of a gun that could shoot hundreds of bullets a minute might make him faint.

Later that afternoon, Mr. Merwyn had us crawling around underneath the Exhibition, clearing out debris that had fallen through the cracks during construction. Mixed in with the dirt and dust and refuse were bits of glass and bent nails, which meant we had to be slow and careful, so we didn't get cut. And since there were only the three of us, we didn't clear a very large area. Mr. Merwyn said it didn't matter, that we'd have plenty of time to clear the rest out after the Exhibition was opened. Despite the prospect of finding coins after that happened, however, none of us were looking forward to it.

By dinner time we were exhausted but, after we ate, we returned to work with the rest of the crew and spent the final hours of daylight putting in the last of the exhibits. As the light grew dim, we made sure we worked inside, and as the workmen gradually left, we moved deeper into the hall, hiding as the security men made their final sweep and locked us in. Knowing we weren't supposed to be there made us nervous and anxious, and it didn't help that the great hall—in the silence of the night—was a spooky place. Eventually, however, well-hidden inside the storeroom, we managed to get some sleep.

◆

The next day was Sunday. We didn't get it off, but we were allowed to sleep late. The sun was already high when Mr. Merwyn came to wake us. When enough men were on site, we slipped out unnoticed and went for breakfast.

When we returned, everyone was called to the central hall. We sat in the seats erected for the opening ceremony and Mr. Paxton walked onto the platform where the officials were to stand. There were a lot of us, but there were so many seats that we didn't fill all of them, and the areas for the orchestra and bands were empty. All of this, along with a huge tree, still didn't take up all the room in the central hall. It was that big.

We weren't the only ones gaping at our surroundings, either. We'd only been there two days, so it was natural for us to be awed, but apparently even those who had worked on the site since the beginning were amazed at what had been constructed. Plus, I expect, this was probably the first time they had been allowed to sit and admire their work.

The buzz of the crowd subsided as Mr. Paxton addressed us.

He thanked us for our hard work and congratulated us on a job well done, but then told us we were behind schedule. There were still exhibits to set up, cleaning to be done and a million and one final touches to put in place to make the Exhibition Hall as stunning as possible when the first visitors arrived. Many of the workers, he told us, had been released, and it was up to us few who remained (though "few" wasn't a word I would have used; there were hundreds of us) to see the project through to completion. And opening the Exhibition, he reminded us, was just the beginning. In the coming months, we would all have to work hard to keep the Hall clean, secure (here, he looked at Morgan, who was sitting in the front row) and in good repair. The eyes of the world would be upon us, and it was up to us to make our country proud.

I wasn't sure how we had ended up in this group—through oversight, error, or Mr. Merwyn's intervention—but I was proud to be part of it. We were then released, and, thanks to Mr. Paxton's pep talk, we all worked twice as hard. We set up last-minute exhibits, helped the landscapers dig, and carted soil away in wooden wheelbarrows, and swept and swept and swept and dusted and dusted and dusted. For a day of rest, we were pretty tired by the time the sun was going down.

As the workers left for home, we kept busy inside the hall, but then Morgan popped up again.

"What are you three doing here?" he barked.

We all jumped and looked guilty, as if he had caught us doing something wrong, which, in a sense, he had.

"Working," John said.

"I mean, why are you still on site?" he asked, his eyes narrowing. "You should have left with the rest of the rabble?"

"We were kept on," I said.

"Well, I didn't approve that," he said. "I'll be seeing Mr. Paxton about this, and I'll have you off this site by sundown."

None of us knew what to say, only that we shouldn't tell him that sundown was happening as he spoke. Then Mr. Merwyn came by, pushing his broom.

"Ah, there you are," he said to us, ignoring Morgan. "You are needed to help install an exhibit in corridor C2." He turned to Morgan. "And I noticed one of the security doors in the main hallway has been modified to allow it to open without a key. I left it that way because I wasn't sure if it was something you had authorized."

Morgan looked flustered. "This better not be your doing," he said to us, and stalked off.

Charlie shook his head in disgust. "Sheesh! He won't rest until he's pinned something on us."

"Thanks for rescuing us," I said to Mr. Merwyn. "But what's he going to do when he finds there's nothing wrong with the security door."

Mr. Merwyn rested his chin on the end of his broom. "Oh, there really is something wrong with the door. Someone has modified it."

"Why would anyone do that?" John asked.

"Why, indeed," Mr. Merwyn said, sweeping his way back down the hall. "Go now. And be vigilant."

# Chapter 20

## Charlie

"He told us to be vigilant," I said.

John still wasn't convinced. "But that doesn't mean we should sleep in the main hall. We'll be caught for sure. We need to sleep here." To emphasize the point, he laid on the floor and wrapped up in a blanket.

"We won't all be asleep," Mitch said. "One of us will be keeping watch."

"Keep watch here."

"It's too far away from everything," I said. "We need to be in a central location."

"I'm not moving."

"Okay. Me and Mitch will keep watch in the main hall. You can stay here. Alone."

Grudgingly, John got to his feet, clutching his blanket to his chest. "All right. Let's go."

We felt our way down the corridors, going by memory, bumping into walls.

"It's darker than the inside of a cow," John said.

"It should be light in the main hall," I said. "At least light enough to see your hand in front of your face."

During the day it takes us about ten minutes to walk from one end of the Exhibition Hall to the other, but in the inky darkness, trying to be silent, it took the better part of an hour. At last, we began to see grey shapes as the darkness, lit by starlight and the crescent moon shining through the ceiling. That made it less scary, but more spooky, if that makes sense. Now we could see dark shapes in the grey light, and hear the soft rustling of rats, while around us and above us loomed the black skeleton of the iron structure.

"See," John said, "nothing here." His voice, barely a whisper, echoed in the huge silence. "Now let's find a place to sleep."

"Wait," Mitch said. "What was that?"

"Just a rat," John said. "Let's get some sleep."

"No," I said, "listen."

The sound came again. A quiet rattle that grew louder and more urgent, then stopped.

"Which direction did it come from?" I asked.

"I can't tell," Mitch said. "There's too many echoes in here."

The sound came again. Louder, followed by a few thumps.

"This way."

We skirted around the seating platform and the stage until we could see the far wall, where the silhouette of a man stood, peering into the hall through the glass of a small, side door.

"Do you think that's the security door Mr. Merwyn told Morgan about?" I asked.

"I think it must be," Mitch said. "And I think that's the guy who fiddled with it."

"I expect he's disappointed," John said.

"Or very frustrated," I added.

"What a dumb thing, though," Mitch said. "How can you make this place secure? It's made of glass. All anyone has to do is throw a rock—"

Crash.

The sound shattered the silence, along with the panel of glass next to the locked door.

The figure ran inside, and I recognized the dark shape by the way it moved.

"That's Farran!"

"He's going for the Talisman," Mitch said. "We have to stop him."

"If he finds out we're here," I said, "he'll tell the police."

"Well, we have to do something!"

"Stop him," John shouted in a deep voice. "He's heading to the left. You men, cut him off!"

Farran stopped and whirled around, looking into the darkness.

"Make some noise, for pity's sake," John hissed.

We ran back around the stage, where we wouldn't be seen, but we stomped as hard as we could to make sure he heard us.

"There he is," I shouted, making my voice as deep as I could.

"Over there," John shouted.

Farran turned, looking left, then right, then in front.

"This way," Mitch shouted.

We stomped our feet, moving just a little closer so he couldn't get a good look at us. That did it. He turned and ran, ducking through the hole he had made in the wall. From outside we heard distant shouting, as Morgan's security men, finally alert to the trouble, came rushing forward, far too late to catch him.

We retreated into the shadows, listening to the

security men as they examined the damage and speculated on their chances of catching the intruder if they ran after him.

"We should go," John said. "They may investigate. If they catch us here …"

"Yeah," I said. "They'll keep watch for us. We'll go back to the storeroom."

"And sleep," Mitch said.

John picked up his blanket. "Finally."

# Chapter 21
## Monday, 28 April 1851

## Mitch

The next morning, we told Mr. Merwyn what had happened. He wasn't surprised, and commended us for our initiative. Then he told us to remain vigilant, industrious and ready for what lay ahead, though he didn't tell us what that might be. And then he disappeared, leaving us to get on with our day.

"Your Druid friend doesn't say much," John observed as we ate a meagre breakfast.

"Yeah," Charlie said. "He's enigmatic."

We started on our usual tasks, which mostly involved sweeping and cleaning, but in the early afternoon, a thin man with a stubbled beard and a fedora came looking for us. He told us his name was Mr. Giovanni and then asked, in a thick Italian accent, "You glaziers?"

"Pardon?"

"Glaziers?"

Both Charlie and I stood staring at him, not understanding.

"He wants to know if we are glass cutters."

Charlie pulled his glass cutter from his pocket. "Yes," he said, holding it up for him to inspect.

Then he looked at me. "You?"

I showed him my cutter. "Yes," I said, "but not so

much."

"You come with me," he said. "All of you."

We followed him outside, to a building on the edge of the grounds. Inside were pallets of plate glass and large worktables. He swept his hand to indicate the empty room. "Most glaziers gone. Job done. Finish." Then he picked up a large plate of glass and laid it on the nearest table. "But work not done. Fix." He spread his hands in front of his face and made a sound like, "Phisssh."

"The broken glass?" Charlie asked.

"Si."

He set about measuring the glass with a long, metal ruler. Then he turned to Charlie. "You cut."

John smiled. "Here's your chance."

Charlie grimaced. "I didn't really think I'd have to do this."

He stepped forward and eyed up the glass. Mr. Giovanni had clamped the metal ruler in place, so Charlie began scoring the glass. Mr. Giovanni watched closely, shaking his head. "No." He took Charlie's hand and moved it and the cutter to a different position. "Now."

Charlie finished scoring the glass and then tapped the cut. It broke cleanly. Charlie grinned. Mr. Giovanni rubbed his stubble and nodded. Then he pointed at me. "Now you."

I tried to make the cut the way he had shown Charlie, but even with Mr. Giovanni helping me I managed to shatter the glass. At least he didn't get angry, he just shrugged and turned to John. "You cut."

John shook his head. "I'm not a glazier."

Mr. Giovanni nodded, then reached out and

squeezed John's bicep with a calloused hand. "But you strong. You come."

Since I couldn't cut glass or lift heavy pallets, I went back into the Exhibition Hall and continued sweeping. I didn't mind; at least I was good at it.

The hall buzzed with activity but in such a large space it didn't feel crowded, and I often found myself on my own, which suited me fine. This was our fourth day working at the Exhibition, so I knew the routine and knew what needed to be done. I pitched in and helped where I could, sometimes with other workers, sometimes by myself. Since I didn't have a boss, as long as I kept busy, no one bothered me or told me what to do. Except Mr. Morgan.

"What do you think you're doing?" he barked, making me jump.

"Working," I said.

"And where's the rest of your gang of thieves?"

I rolled my eyes, then stopped sweeping and turned to face him. "I don't know of any gang of thieves," I said, "but Charlie and John are helping Mr. Giovanni fix the broken panels."

Morgan snorted. "All these workers here, loyal, honest, English workers, and he picks transient vagabonds for helpers."

It wasn't really a question, but I answered it anyway. "Charlie and I are glaziers," I said. "That's why he wanted our help."

"Glaziers!" He gave a sharp laugh. "That's why you're here pushing a broom?"

I turned away and continued sweeping, both so he couldn't see me turn red and to encourage him to end the conversation. I glanced around, hoping to see Mr. Merwyn, who often turned up at these times, but it appeared I was on my own.

I heard his footsteps come up behind me then felt the blow on the side of my head. I staggered sideways, dropping my broom but managed to stay on my feet. I turned to face him, still red, but from anger, not embarrassment.

"Don't you turn your back on me, boy," he screamed, his face, also very red, so close to mine I could feel the spit flying.

My mind reeled. He was clearly looking for a fight now that there was only one of us. But attacking him would not be a wise thing to do. What would Mr. Merwyn advise? I drew a breath. "I'm sorry, Mr. Morgan," I said. "I won't do it again."

The apology seemed to disarm him. He narrowed his eyes. "See that you don't," he said, and stalked off.

I rubbed the side of my head, picked up my broom and began sweeping in the opposite direction. After I put enough space between us, I put the encounter behind me and concentrated on my tasks, counting myself lucky that I had gotten off so lightly.

There were only two working days left, and the activity was furious. Throughout the length of the Hall people were putting the finishing touches on the exhibits and the interior designs and, whether I could see anyone or not, there was the feeling of activity wherever I went. But as I moved further toward the far end, I was disturbed from my meticulous dusting of a statue featuring a naked woman feeding a lion, by an alarming sensation of isolation.

This section of the Hall was quiet and still. Had Morgan tricked me into wandering into a deserted area, so he could attack me without any witnesses present? Concerned and a little bit frightened, I put my back to the statue and scanned the cluttered hall. It seemed empty, and except for the distant sound of workmen, silent. Then I heard footsteps.

I tensed. Were they coming my way? Should I make a run for it? Or hide? Then the footsteps stopped. Then they started again. Then I heard the light clatter of someone moving objects around. I started to relax, but only a little. It wasn't Morgan. He would come at me directly. But who was it? Farran? Was he obsessed enough to be nosing around during the day?

I crept forward, hiding behind statues and exhibit stalls, working my way down the corridor until I found the source of the noise: a young girl, playing with an exhibit of huge, ornate chess pieces.

She looked about eleven years old, with dark hair hanging down to her shoulders in ringlets. She wore the most ornate dress I had ever seen on a child—white, ruffled and festooned with ribbons of red and blue—which matched the ribbons in her hair. Despite being a child, she radiated self-confidence, and showed no sign of embarrassment, shame or surprise when she saw me watching her.

"What are you doing?" I asked, keeping my voice low. If there were other people around, I didn't want to get her into trouble. As it was, I could just put the pieces back and clean any fingerprints off them. So, no harm done, assuming she left.

But, instead, she stared at me with a look somewhere between amazement and anger. "Did you speak to me?"

"Yes," I said. "You can't be in there. You're going to get in trouble."

Her dark eyes widened, then narrowed. "How dare

121

you!"

I walked to the edge of the exhibit and folded my arms. "How dare I what?"

The girl looked startled for a moment. "Talk to me. Presume to tell me what to do."

I shook my head. "All right, have your fun. But if someone catches you in there, you're going to be in trouble."

I started the walk away, but the girl called to me. Commanded, really. "Do not turn your back on me."

"What is it with you? Who do you think you are that you can wander in and do as you please?"

She pulled herself up to her full height and looked so self-assured that I began to think I was the one in over my head. "Papa built this palace," she said.

"Oh," I said, immediately changing my tone. I even removed my cap. "I'm sorry. You're Mr. Paxton's daughter, then?"

She laughed, but in a way that made me feel stupid. "The gardener? Do you speak in jest, or with intent to insult?"

I put my cap back on. "Look, I don't care who you are, you've got to get out of there before you break something."

"I told you," she said, displaying real anger for the first time. "Papa made this." She waved her arms as if to encompass the entire exhibition. "And I can do as I please." A look of malicious mischief crossed her face. "And if I want to tip this queen over, I will."

She started pushing a chess piece that was taller than her, made of marble and intricately carved. If it fell, it would be ruined. I jumped up on the chess board, dodging around the pieces, and grabbed for the falling queen. It was heavy, but I stopped it in mid-tumble and stood it back up.

"That's enough," I said. "Time to go."

I laid my hand on the middle of her back to guide her off the board. And she screamed.

She screamed as if a hot iron had been pressed to her back instead of my hand. She screamed as if the world's largest, hairiest, ugliest spider just dropped down in front of her. She screamed so loud I was afraid the glass would shatter.

Startled, I scurried away from her and fell off the edge of the marble base into the corridor. Seconds later six uniformed men surrounded me, five rifles pointed at my face, and a sabre poked against my throat. But at least the girl stopped screaming.

A man wearing knee-length boots, white pants and a red jacket decked out in gold buttons and braids dashed toward us. He jumped up onto the chessboard and scooped the girl into his arms.

"Minyouveel," he said. "Minyouveel, what has happened? Are you hurt? What did the shirker do?"

Still holding the girl, he walked gracefully through the chess pieces and stepped down into the corridor. The ring of soldiers opened for him, their rifles on their shoulders and the sabre back in its scabbard. Both he and the girl glared at me.

"He touched me," the girl wailed.

"Schurke!" the man said, as he kicked me in the side.

"What the hell?" I tried to sit up, but the rifles returned. "I'm not a shirker," I said.

The man glared at me. "Schurke!" he said again. "Villain!"

I shook my head. "Look, I was working. I was just trying to keep her from ruining that exhibit."

123

I pointed at the girl. The soldiers looked alarmed. The man put the girl down and she stood next to him, a smirk on her face.

"You will address us properly." He said it in a tone that suggested he was going to kick me again, but he didn't, he just looked at me as if I was expected to say something.

"Well, okay," I said after an awkward pause. "So, who are you?"

The soldiers gasped.

"Insolent hund!" the man said. He still didn't kick me; he just pointed to a soldier and the soldier kicked me.

I gripped my side and moaned. "Okay," I gasped. "I'm sorry. Whatever I did, I didn't mean it. Can I just go back to work now?"

"I am Prince Albert," the man said. "And this is Her Royal Highness the Princess Victoria. Now stand and address us properly."

I got up, still clutching my ribs, and faced them. I didn't need to remove my cap; it was on the floorboards.

"Forgive me," I said, making what I hoped was a suitable bow. "Your Royal Highness Princess Victoria, I meant no offense."

Albert's lip curled. "You should be proud to work in this temple of progress," he said, "but instead you bring shame on your family."

"My family's back home in America. And I didn't do anything they'd be ashamed of. Your Royal Highness."

Albert looked at me like I was something he didn't want to step in. "A foreigner," he said, spitting the word out, which I thought was a bit rich coming from him in his heavily accented English. He took his child's hand. "Come, Minyouveel," he said. And, after a few sneaky shoves from the soldiers as they followed Albert and the Princess, I was alone again.

I picked up my cap and broom and began fixing the chessboard, wishing, for the first time, that I had been chosen to work with Charlie.

# Chapter 22

## Charlie

I felt bad that Mitch had to go off and work on his own, but then, after hastily explaining what I was expected to do, Mr. Giovanni took John, and the panel of glass, to the Exhibition Hall, leaving me alone in the workroom, so it appeared we were all working on our own.

My job was to cut more glass for other panels that needed replacing. I laid out a glass sheet, glad Mr. Giovanni wasn't watching, and tried to score and cut it. Naturally, it broke in the wrong place. So did the second one. Then I panicked, until I found where the rest of them were stored. There were pallets of them, which was a good thing, because I broke the third one too.

This time, though, I stayed calm. They weren't coming back until they fixed the damaged door and finished their inspection of the Exhibition Hall, looking for damage. That was going to take hours, so I concentrated hard on the next one, taking my time to get the score-mark perfect. At last, I got the hang of it, and the glass broke cleanly. I made the second, more difficult, lengthwise cut and began breathing easier when that one, too, was successful. A panel, trimmed to the correct size, now lay on the table.

It got easier after that, and I worked in silence,

alone in the big room, for another hour or two. When I finished, I stacked the cut glass, and removed the broken pieces, adding them to the growing pile. I didn't want Mr. Giovanni to see how many panels I had ruined, so I found a wheelbarrow and carefully loaded the broken glass into it. Then I wheeled it outside, looking for a place to dump it.

With the opening ceremony three days away, the place no longer looked like a building site. The lawns were manicured, the shrubs planted, the fencing installed. There were still a few crates around, but they were being cleared out, as well as the work sheds. The one I was working in was due to be dismantled the next day, and the glass repair shop moved to a location inside the Hall. There were no piles of rubbish where the glass wouldn't look out of place, and wheeling it down to the other end and just leaving it there wouldn't work because there were fancy carriages and important looking men, and lots of uniformed guards carrying rifles, milling around. It looked as if someone important was visiting, and I couldn't see pushing a wheelbarrow of broken glass through that throng.

Then I saw a shed, not far away in the other direction. They'd be taking it down soon, but I could at least park the wheelbarrow in it for now, until I figured out what to do with it. I looked around. The place was busy, but no one was looking at me, so I walked as nonchalantly as I could to the shed and looked inside. It was a jumble of cut off pieces of lumber, iron bars, broken carts and even broken glass. Perfect.

I pushed the barrow inside and pulled the door closed. Two dirty windows allowed enough light in

127

for me to guide the wheelbarrow around the piles of junk. I pushed it next to where the glass was. Then, as I was about to dump it, the door opened. I spun around and saw a man in a bowler hat who was, thankfully, looking over his shoulder. I stifled a gasp and jumped to the side, hiding behind a stack of boards.

I calmed my breathing and listened, hoping the man would find what he wanted and leave, but he walked in, closed the door and waited. Soon, the door opened again. More footsteps. The door closed and one of the men spoke.

"Did anyone see you?" The voice was brisk, business-like.

"No."

My heart jumped in my chest. It was Morgan.

"Everything is in place?"

"Yes. The Prince is here this afternoon, inspecting his creation. He will return tomorrow morning, with less of an entourage. And less security."

"And the jewel?"

"Here as well."

"You can provide a window?"

Morgan hesitated slightly. "Yes. For the price we agreed."

A few murmurs, then a rustle of paper and clink of coins.

"This is not—"

"Half now," the man said. "The other half when we are successful." His tone encouraged no negotiation.

Another hesitation. "No one gets hurt, right?"

"We are men of principle, Mr. Morgan, not murderers. Keep your end of the bargain and all will be well."

Muffled clicking as Morgan put the money in his pocket. "All right. Eleven o'clock. Tomorrow morning. You'll have five, maybe ten minutes."

"That will be sufficient."

The door opened and closed. I held my breath. One of the men was still in the shed. Footsteps, a rattle of iron, the thumping of wood. It had to be Morgan, not wanting to be seen with the other man, now waiting and looking for anything worth stealing. The sounds grew closer. Glass crunched.

"Hell-o, what's this?"

I nearly screamed, but he hadn't found me.

"What lazy bugger left this here?"

A crash of glass as Morgan dumped the barrow's load, then his footsteps, and the squeaking of the barrow's wheel, retreated toward the door. Then I was alone.

I stayed hidden for another five minutes, until I could breathe, and my heart stopped racing, then I went back to the workroom, leaving the shed and walking as if nothing had happened. No one took notice of me, and Morgan was nowhere in sight.

# Chapter 23

## Mitch

"You'll never guess what happened to me!"

"You'll never guess what I heard!"

"You'll never guess what I did."

We spoke all at once, as soon as we met up to go to dinner.

"Seriously, you have to hear mine first."

Again, all at once.

In the end, we drew straws and Charlie and I had to wait while John described his day.

"We climbed on top of the Palace," he said. "Mr. Giovani showed me how to get up there, and there's walkways and tracks on the roof so panels can be repaired. And they open and close to let air out, or keep it in. It's amazing. And it's so big! We went from one end to the other, inspecting all the glass. It took hours."

"Well, that explains why you never came back," Charlie said. "I cut fifty sheets of glass, and then had to leave them piled on the tables."

"You'll need to cut more tomorrow, then," John said. "We marked out sixty-seven panels that need replacing."

"We can't do that much in two days," Charlie said.

John shook his head. "There are fitters, men who can replace panels. Mr. Giovanni just needed someone to cut the glass because the replacement sheets didn't come in the right size."

"You mean he needed a slave to do his work for him," Charlie said, still grousing about being left alone all afternoon.

"Well, you gotta hear mine now," I said. "I met Prince Albert, and the Princess Victoria."

"I saw them, as well," John said, not as impressed as I thought he would be. "From above. They looked like ants, crawling around the exhibits. The Prince, the Palace Guards, and the others."

"Well, I met them," I said. "I talked to them."

Hearing that, John became truly impressed. "My Lord! What were they like? Were they as grand as people say?"

I hesitated, not wanting to dampen the shine on my story.

"They were very regal," I said. "Very much in charge." John looked eager for more, so I pressed on, carefully avoiding the unpleasant parts. "They're very devoted to each other. He calls her 'Minyooveel' and I thought that was kinda human. For a King."

"He's not a king!" John said.

I shrugged while Charlie fidgeted impatiently. When silence returned, he smirked, and said, "There's going to be a robbery, tomorrow morning at eleven o'clock. And Morgan is organizing it."

We gasped and stood open-mouthed as Charlie recounted what he had heard while hiding in a shed.

"What do you think it all means?" John asked, after Charlie finished.

"I don't know," Charlie said, "other than they want to steal this jewel."

"Why do they want Morgan to get them a

window? They're surrounded by them."

"I think they mean a window of opportunity," I said. "Morgan will make sure his security men are looking somewhere else when they do the robbery."

"And we know when that's going to happen," John said. "We can stop it."

"But we don't know what they want to steal."

John looked exasperated. "The jewel."

"But there are hundreds of them," Charlie said. "We can't guard them all."

"It will be the Koh-i-noor."

"The core-innor? What's that?"

John rolled his eyes. "Only the biggest diamond in the world. Mr. Giovanni told me about it. They are installing it tomorrow morning and inviting lots of dignitaries to view it."

"If there will be that many people there," I said, "then they won't be able to steal it."

"Unless Morgan helps them," Charlie said. "He's going to give them the opportunity. Somehow."

"So, what do we do?" John asked. "We can't go to the police, and we can't even tell the head of security."

"What about Mr. Paxton?"

Charlie thought for a second, then shook his head. "He'd only tell Morgan. Or the police. And they'd want to talk to us."

John sighed and put his head in his hands. "I suppose, then, we should just let them steal it."

"We can't do that," I sputtered.

John looked up. "Why not. It doesn't really concern us. All you really care about is that Talisman thing. Maybe we should just forget about this and—"

"But what if it is the Talisman," I said. "They

could be using a code word."

Charlie's eyes widened. "That's right! And Farran is a friend of Morgan. He might have hired some thieves to steal it for him and arranged for Morgan to make it possible. And if everyone is somewhere else gaping at this core-nore diamond—"

"Koh-i-noor," John said.

"—that will provide him with a golden opportunity."

"We need to protect the Talisman," I said.

Charlie nodded. "And we need to tell Mr. Merwyn."

We found Mr. Merwyn, as usual, in the storeroom, which had become a sort of office. Since the speech on Sunday, and the shift from construction to maintenance, Mr. Merwyn was now in charge of a lot more people, and so busy we hardly saw him. We interrupted him while he was sitting at a makeshift desk, writing in a ledger.

He listened without comment to Charlie's story. His shaggy eyebrows knitted together when we told him our theory about Farran.

"That is disturbing," Mr. Merwyn said when we finished. Then he rested his bearded chin on his hands and stared beyond us, as if concentrating on something in the far distance. "Whatever Mr. Morgan's conspirators are up to, the danger remains. The Talisman must be protected at all costs. It must be returned to you, and you must carry it to the Tor, to reinstate it in its proper place."

"We will," I said, even though I had no idea how that might happen.

Mr. Merwyn shook his head. "I see a decision, a conundrum, an impossible choice. And yet, it must be made."

"What is it."

He looked at me, his eyes glistening. "I know not. Something stands in the way, and I cannot see beyond it. But I sense a darkness, and it makes my heart tremble. I have seen kingdoms destroyed, empires rise and fall, plagues and pestilence sweep over the Land like a scythe, but never have I sensed a darkness like the one I fear is coming. I cannot know if the Land follows the path of light or plunges into darkness. All I know is, you must make a choice. And the fate of the Talisman, the fate of the Land, rests upon it."

"But we don't know what to do," Charlie said. "We need your help."

Mr. Merwyn sighed. "I cannot provide the assistance you desire. This is your quest. My involvement may cause more ill than good."

"But—"

Mr. Merwyn held up his hand. "If there does come a time when you truly need help. Seek the Talisman. Go to it, wherever it is. And I will be there."

"That's it?" Charlie asked. "That's all you've got to say?"

Mr Merwyn turned back to his ledger and dipped his pen in the inkwell. "That is all I can offer. Pray it does not come to that. Now go and protect the Talisman. The rest will take care of itself."

We left him and returned to work.

"So," Charlie said, once we were back in the main corridor, "no pressure, then?"

# Chapter 24
## Tuesday, 29 April 1851

## Charlie

That was how, the next day at twenty minutes to eleven, me and John found ourselves hiding in an exhibit of chimney ornaments, watching two men continuously sweeping the corridor in front of the glass case the Talisman was displayed in.

Mr. Merwyn was with us, and he wasn't letting us just sit and watch. He had us dusting and polishing and sweeping, and making sure the chimney ornaments shone. It was annoying, but I suppose it was for the best. If someone came by, it would look less suspicious if we were working rather than crouching behind the exhibits staring at the sweepers.

As it happened, no one did come by, and as the hour drew near, we paid more attention to the Talisman and less to our cleaning. At eleven o'clock, the corridor was still empty. At eleven thirty, with the window of opportunity long closed, we decided no one was coming. Then I heard footsteps.

I motioned for John to hide, and we ducked behind a plinth. The footsteps came closer, fast and stealthy, and stopped right in front of our exhibit. I peeked around the plinth.

"It's Farran!"

John waved at Mr. Merwyn to get his attention,

then pointed toward the corridor.

I took another peek. John squeezed up beside me. "What's he doing?"

"Nothing. He's just standing there, watching the guys sweeping. Now he's pretending to look at an exhibit. I think he's hoping they'll go away."

Mr. Merwyn stepped into the hallway. "Can I help you, sir?"

Farran jumped like he'd been poked with an electric prod, then spun around. When he saw Mr. Merwyn, he relaxed, and drew himself up to his full height. "No, I do not. I am merely having a look around."

"Are you with the Royal entourage? I believe they are gathered in the Transept for a viewing of the Koh-i-noor diamond. If you hurry, you may still see it."

"Am I …? No. As I said, I'm just looking."

"Do you work here?"

Farran puffed his chest. "Do not presume to interrogate me—"

Mr. Merwyn remain unfazed. "The Exhibition doesn't open to the public until the first of May. If you are not an official visitor, or employed by Mr. Paxton, I'm going to have to ask you to leave."

"How dare you speak to me like that."

Now the other two sweepers approached, and Farran found himself surrounded.

"I am your better," Farran sputtered. "You cannot treat me like this."

"I'm sorry, sir," Mr. Merwyn continued, his voice still low and courteous. "The public are not allowed in. We'll escort you to the exit."

Farran's face went purple. "You will do no such

thing!"

"This looks heavy, sir," one of the other men said, reaching for the bag in Farran's hand. "Shall I carry this for you?"

Farran tried to pull the bag away, but the man snatched it from him.

"Help," Farran shouted. "I'm being robbed."

The man made no reaction. He reached into Farran's bag and pulled out a brick. "Ah, sir, I see why your bag is so heavy. Someone put a brick in it."

"I don't know what that is," Farran said. "I never saw—"

"What's going on here!" Pounding footsteps. "You men, leave that gentleman be!"

"Morgan," I said. "What's he doing here?"

John shifted beside me, trying to get a look. "Coming to help Farran steal your Talisman, I expect."

The man holding the brick slipped it back into the bag and held it out to Farran. "You'll be wanting this back, sir."

Farran pushed his hand away. "I told you, I've never seen that before."

"Mr. Farran," Morgan said as he rushed up to the group, "what are you doing here?"

"Well, I'm just—"

Morgan didn't wait for his answer. "And you men, what do you think you're doing?"

"We're cleaning," Mr. Merwyn said. "And this gentleman appeared lost, so we were helping him find the exit."

Morgan looked at Farran. "Is that true?"

Farran looked around, trying to avoid eye contact with anyone and, failing that, turned his gaze to the floor. "Well, I … it seemed … I was just looking … looking around. And these men—"

"Mr. Farran," Morgan said, struggling to remain calm, "I was happy to show you around the other day, but we're on a tight schedule, and the public are not yet invited in."

"I was just … I meant no harm."

"You'll have to leave," Morgan said. "I'll show you the way." Then Morgan turned to the other men. "You! Back to work or I'll see you out as well. Permanently"

The men stepped back, and Morgan motioned for Farran to follow, his face pinched with controlled rage, as if he wanted to yell at Farran but didn't dare, because he was a lower rank. Some sort of class thing.

The two workmen—one still carrying Farran's bag—took the opportunity to escape in the opposite direction, but Mr. Merwyn continued to sweep. He didn't glance at us as he pushed his broom— appearing unconcerned about the incident or the Talisman—slowly down the corridor, following Morgan and Farran as they marched out of sight. Soon, silence and solitude returned to the great hall, and when we thought it was safe, we came out of hiding and caught up with Mr. Merwyn.

"I told you they were plotting to steal your Talisman," John said.

Mr. Merwyn, looking thoughtful, nodded. "Then why was he not successful?"

That was typical of Mr. Merwyn; never an answer, always a question."

"Well, because we were there."

"But what was it Charlie heard?"

"He came at the wrong time," I said, as I saw what

Mr Merwyn was getting at. "And Morgan was supposed to have the location cleared. He would have made sure we weren't there. And he seemed genuinely surprised to see Farran."

Mr. Merwyn stopped and sat on a railing. He had led us back to the Talisman exhibit.

"And what do you make of all that?" he asked.

"They weren't talking about the Talisman," I said.

John looked dejected, then he brightened. "But if you hadn't heard them, and I hadn't thought that, we wouldn't have been here guarding it." He looked at Mr. Merwyn. "So, it all worked out for the best, even though we were wrong."

"Then we weren't forewarned," I said. "We were just lucky. Again."

Mr. Merwyn nodded. "The Talisman makes its own luck. You were wise to follow your instincts."

Confident that Farran was gone and concerned that Morgan might come back, we re-joined the other men and boys working to get the great hall ready for Thursday's opening.

"I wonder what they were really after," John said as we broke for lunch.

I looked around at the others, eating, chatting, trying to catch a nap, and felt a vague unease. "Yeah," I said. "And where's Mitch?"

# Chapter 25

## Mitch

It was just about eleven o'clock when I figured it out.

I decided not to help guard the Talisman. Mr. Merwyn and some of his workmen had that under control. If anything did happen—aside from an armed assault—they would be able to handle it. And we weren't even able to help because, if Farran turned up, he'd see us, so the three of us were supposed to hide. And just watch. Charlie and John could do that just as well if I was there or not.

So, I left them to it, and went to check on the Jewel, the Koh-i-noor, which had to be what Morgan's gang were really after.

Usually, when we walked around and other people were there, we kept to the side corridors off the main hallway, as they were often empty. But not this day. The corridors, and the main hallway, were buzzing, so I went down the middle and just tried to not run into too many people while I kept an eye out for Farran. When I got to the centre of the exhibition hall, I found the north transept packed. I assumed that was where the diamond was, because a crowd of people had surrounded something that looked like a giant birdcage with a golden crown on top. Men in top hats jostled for a view of whatever was in the cage. Others stood to the side, posing in front of a man peering into a big box that I supposed was a camera.

It looked like the diamond was well-guarded, despite what Morgan had promised. But then, I didn't know for sure if it was the diamond they were looking at. I moved a little closer and nearly ran into a tall man holding a silver-tipped cane and wearing a suit with ruffles down the front and ridiculously long tails in the back. He walked straight at me, as if I wasn't there, and I had to jump out of his way to avoid a collision.

"Excuse me," I said, as he strode by.

He stopped. "Did you speak?"

"Yes," I said.

"To me?"

"I almost ran into you," I said, even though it had been the other way round, "and I apologized."

I didn't know what I expected, but I didn't expect him to swing his cane at me.

"Hey," I shouted. "What the hell?"

The man, his bearded face set in a grimace, swung again. "How dare you speak to me." And again. "I'll see you given the sack." And again. "I'll see you jailed." And again. "I'll see you hanged."

I kept dodging away, and each time he missed he seemed to get angrier. I figured I'd better get away before he had me in front of a firing squad or got so angry that he drew attention. I made one last dodge as he swung his cane, then darted around him, ran toward the nearly empty South Transept, and ducked into a smaller corridor, past the Canadian and West Indies exhibits.

The man didn't chase me, but I heard him—above the babble of the main hall—shouting for a police officer. I decided it would be best if I went back to where Charlie and John were hiding and help them watch the Talisman. The Koh-i-noor might be in danger, but I no longer cared; these people were crazy. I started down the corridor, then saw two other men, and one of them was Albert.

I jumped to the side, next to a sculpture exhibit, hoping he wouldn't notice me. I wondered why he was strolling down an empty corridor, apparently on friendly terms with a man who was not royalty. His companion wore no hat, and his wiry hair stood out from his head, reflecting his unkempt beard and moustache. He was also dressed in a brown suit and jacket that looked like it had seen better days, and he wore a yellow cravat bunched at this throat. Albert, on the other hand, wore a top hat, starched white shirt and a severe black suit with tails. Then I realized it wasn't Albert, just someone who looked a lot like him. This gave me hope that they would pass by without looking my way.

"I agree it is utterly marvellous," the bearded man said. "But I do wonder at the cost."

"Less zan you think," the man in the top hat said. His accent was so much like Albert's that I took an involuntary step back, while giving him a second look to be certain I wasn't mistaken.

"Still, it's a bit ostentatious," the bearded man continued. "All this wealth, while we are surrounded by crushing poverty, don't you think?"

Top Hat laughed. "I think you think too much. This exhibition is to show off your technology, your riches, not your poor."

"Riches, yes, but presented poorly. That diamond, the Koh-i-noor, what a disgraceful setting. It looks like a walnut in a gilded cage."

"Ja. There I agree with you. It makes it look so small, even though it is large."

"And ugly."

Top Hat laughed again. "Ugly, ja. But ich hätte nichts dagegen, wenn es mein Juwel."

"Minyouveel," I thought. Then, without thinking, said, "What did you say?"

Top Hat glared at me. "Unverschämter Hund!"

"Sorry," I said, backing away so he couldn't get at me quickly. "But what does minyouveel mean?"

Top Hat glared harder and seemed like he might come after me, but his companion put a hand on his arm and smiled. "Are you American?"

I nodded.

"Ah, Americans! Such fine people. Is my German friend confusing you?"

Top Hat continued to glare at me, and at the other man, who still had a hold on his arm.

I stared blankly at them. Then the bearded man laughed. "Do you have a name?"

"Mitch."

"Mitch," he said, pulling a notepad from inside his jacket. "What a superb name. And what brings you to this grand exhibition?"

I shrugged. "I work here."

"How extraordinary," the man said, scribbling in his notepad.

"Not, really," I said. "I just want to know—"

"Not extraordinary! You travelled thousands of miles to find work. And look at you!" He released his friend and lurched forward grabbing me by the shoulder. "Grimy from head to foot. Lean and wiry. Are they working you hard?"

I nodded. He let me go and scribbled some more.

"How much are they paying you?"

"They're not paying me," I said. "I just get whatever money I find that falls through the cracks."

The man's eyes lit up. He seemed to shake with excitement. "How astonishing! I must put you in a book!"

Once again, he opened his notepad and began scribbling.

Top Hat leaned forward. "Herr Dickens, ve must movf on. The official unveiling begins."

Mr. Dickens grabbed my hand and pumped it enthusiastically. "How marvellous to meet you, young Mitch."

Mr. Dickens dropped my hand and re-joined Top Hat. Then he made a small bow in my direction. "Good-day, young man. A pleasure to meet you."

Mr. Dickens smiled, but Top Hat scowled, clearly disappointed that he hadn't been allowed to thump me.

"But minyouveel," I said as they turned away, "what does that mean?"

Mr. Dickens looked over his shoulder. "It means, my jewel."

They walked away together, with Mr. Dickens muttering to himself. "How marvellous, the confusion over language, what a motif, and the accent, so captivating …"

I watched them go. When they left the corridor and entered the Transept, I continued toward Charlie and John and the Talisman, thinking.

Minyouveel meant "My Jewel." So that was what Albert called his daughter. And then it hit me like a physical jolt.

"They're not after any jewels," I said out loud. "They're after the Princess."

But what could I do about it? I couldn't go to the police, or Morgan, and Albert would probably have me thrown in prison if he saw me again. Mr. Merwyn? He'd at least know where to begin. Then the other thought hit me: I didn't have time to go to anyone. The robbery was to take place at eleven o'clock, the same time as the unveiling of the diamond, which meant it was going to happen now, and I had no idea where the Princess was. I took a few more steps, feeling hopeless. I knew what was going to happen and when, but I didn't know where, so I couldn't do a thing about it. Another step. But I did have an idea where it might happen.

I started running before the thought even completed itself. The chessboard. That's where she would be. I raced down the corridor, across the nearly empty South Transept, sparing only a glance at the North Transept and the ceremony, before dashing past the offices and the China exhibit, into the far corridor. It was completely empty, so I ran unimpeded, past linens, plates, furniture and clothing, turning as I passed the Belgium exhibit, rushing down a short connecting corridor and coming out in the main hallway near the chessboard. And there she was, standing amid the pieces, moving them around with a smug smile on her face. I didn't slow. I leapt onto the board, dodged around the pieces, grabbed her by an arm, and pulled her off the other side before she even knew what was happening. And she screamed.

"Good," I shouted, "Scream. Scream for all you're worth."

I dragged her to the corridor and back the way I

145

had come, pulling her behind me, her screams echoing through the huge hall. Then they stopped. Her arm slipped from my grip. I turned. A man had grabbed her from behind. He had his arm around her throat and a hand over her mouth. There was a cloth in his hand, and she appeared to go limp. Before I could even think, a big hand covered my mouth and I was yanked backward into the shadows, along with the Princess.

# Chapter 26

## Charlie

When dinner time drew near and Mitch hadn't returned, I knew something was wrong. Me and John talked to as many maintenance men as we could find, but none of them had seen Mitch, or any unusual activity. It seemed as if he had simply vanished.

That was unlike him, so just before sunset, me and John decided to talk with Mr. Merwyn. But as we walked across the vast entrance hall on our way to the storeroom, where we hoped to find Mr. Merwyn, we were arrested by the Queen's Guards and thrown into the Tower of London.

They weren't very gentle about it, either. They grabbed us by the arms, jerked us off our feet and marched us, with our feet dangling six inches off the ground, into the courtyard. A wagon, with a sturdy oak and metal box on the back, drawn by four horses and surrounded by guards, waited for us. They threw us inside. The door slammed and the wagon lurched forward.

"You alright?" John asked.

I sat up with some difficulty. I was sore, the carriage was dark, and it jolted over the roadway in an alarming manner. We were travelling very fast, for a horse-drawn vehicle, anyway, and the clattering of hooves and the rumbling of the wheels made it difficult to hear.

"I'm fine," I shouted.

We settled as best we could in the bare, tiny space, bouncing up, down, and tossed every which-way, until I thought my bones were going to rattle apart. Then the carriage slowed. We heard voices. More clattering over cobble stones and, finally, it stopped.

The door flew open. I glimpsed grey towers, like castle turrets, against the dim sky, and marching men in brilliant red and gold uniforms. Then a sack was thrown over my head and I was dragged out of the wagon.

I was carried, rather than marched, a short way over a cobbled yard, through a door and up a winding staircase. The next thing I knew, I was lying on a cold, hard floor. Something landed next to me. A door slammed. A bolt clanged shut. Then silence returned.

I pulled the sack off my head and saw John lying next to me. He shook his head and combed his hair with his fingers, then retrieved his cap, which was still in the sack.

"Where are we?" I asked.

We sat up, our backs against a wall. There was only a little light, let in through a narrow slit, but it was enough to see the features of the room, if there had been any. Save for some old straw scattered over the stone floor, which was polished smooth with age, the room was empty. The door—arched and thick and rimmed with iron—was solid except for a small square in the centre that was criss-crossed with metal bars.

"I think I know where we are," John said. "The question is, 'why?'"

I got up and looked through the narrow window.

Below was a huge courtyard surrounded by high stone walls and the turrets I had seen earlier. Soldiers, carrying rifles and pikes, marched below us, amid horses, carts and cannons.

John appeared by my side and peered out. "We're in the Tower of London." He sounded awed and scared. "But what did we do to earn this reward?"

We were left to ponder that for over an hour. We stared out the window, paced, and finally sat back against the wall, still none the wiser. Then the bolts slid back, and the door creaked open.

A man entered and, at first, I thought he might be another prisoner because he was accompanied by two guards. But he was dressed in a red tunic with a high collar, and his wavy black hair, long sideburns and moustache were all neatly trimmed. Also, the soldiers weren't roughing him up. In fact, they kept their distance, as if they were afraid of him. Then, I thought, he might be their superior officer.

He stood in front of us, gazing down with such disgust and anger it made me instantly afraid. One of the soldiers threw something at me. It landed on the floor at my feet. I picked it up. It was Mitch's flat cap.

"Where did you get this?" I asked. "It belongs to my brother. He's missing."

"So, you admit your guilt," the man said, in an accent that reminded me of old World War Two movies. "You have five minutes."

"For what?" I asked.

His balled fists rested on his hips. "To tell me the truth."

I took a breath, trying to remain calm. "The truth about what? This is my brother's hat. That's true. Where did you find it?"

The man sneered. "You already know that. I do not need to tell you. You need to tell me what he has done."

"But I don't know where you found it, and I don't know what he's done. I'm trying to find him."

"Your time is running out."

"It's going to have to run out," I said. "I don't know anything, so I can't tell you anything."

"Then you'll hang."

That did it. I jumped to my feet and pointed my finger in the man's face. "Just who do you think you are? I demand a lawyer. I demand to be let out of here. We're being held without due process. You'll be fired from whatever middle-management position—"

That's as far as I got before the soldiers slammed me up against the wall so hard my teeth rattled.

Then the soldiers dragged John to his feet and shoved him against the wall next to me. His face was white, his eyes wide and his hands trembling.

"How dare you sit in the presence of His Majesty."

As for His Majesty, he stared at me with a look of shock on his face, that deepened when I shouted, "Who the hell are you?"

The room fell silent, then a soldier said. "That is His Majesty, Prince Albert, consort to Her Majesty Victoria, Queen of the United Kingdom of Great Britain and Ireland."

I glared at Albert, who had regained his composure. "Well, I didn't vote for you."

Beside me, John gasped. Albert's eyes narrowed. "You are impatient for the rope, ja?"

"I am impatient with you! I didn't do anything wrong. I don't know anything, so I can't tell you anything. My brother is missing, and I need to look

150

for him. Now let us go."

Albert smirked. "You admit you know of the dastardly plot by your brother, to steal my child. Tell me where she is."

I thought hard. "Mitch didn't steal your daughter," I said. "He met her, he told us that. And he met you. But that was Monday. Today we were … busy."

"Then why was his cap found where my daughter was last seen?"

I slumped against the wall and became so limp the soldiers let me go. "I don't know anything about that."

Albert stepped forward. "Tell me where she is!"

Behind his anger, I sensed desperation, and fear. His need to find his daughter was as deep as my desire to find Mitch.

"If I knew, I'd tell you," I said. "Because whoever has your daughter, has Mitch too."

# Chapter 27

## Mitch

My head ached, my eyes burned, and my parched mouth was bound closed with a gag. Behind my back, my wrist throbbed as they rubbed against the rope binding them. I tried to move my legs, but they too were bound together. I was in a small, dark space, like a horizontal closet, but without a door. Light leaked in through two tiny windows, one on each side, but no air, or sound came in with it. Next to me lay the Princess, so motionless I was afraid she might be dead.

The men who had grabbed her had drugged me too, and that was all I remembered until we both woke up in the tiny room. The Princess, naturally, tried to scream. And when she found she couldn't, she thrashed, flopping in the tight space like a landed fish, which thumped me painfully against the wall. When she finally stopped, she started crying, but that was hard because her mouth was covered, and she kept blowing snot out of her nose and I was afraid she might suffocate. Then she finally went quiet, and I became worried.

I suspected the room was a box of some sort mounted on a wagon because, even though I couldn't hear anything, I could feel the vibration of the wheels and the sway of the carriage. I kept still, breathing slowly, trying to calm myself, listening to see if the Princess was breathing. She was. Her breath was there, shallow, and bubbling through the snot in her nose. She appeared to be asleep, which was fine with me. Whatever it was we were in had obviously been made to hold one person comfortably; I was, in so many ways, excess baggage.

I wondered how long we had been travelling, and how much longer it would go on. I was about ready to pee my pants, and the occasional bumping of the carriage didn't help. Eventually, the Princess began to stir. She blew a gob of snot out of her nose and started banging her head on the wall, grunting through her gag. Tied up and lying down, she couldn't move her head very fast, so I wasn't worried that she'd break her skull—thick as it was—I was just worried about my bladder, and wondered how she'd feel if I pissed all over Her Royal Highness. I looked at her and shook my head, meaning, "No," trying to make her understand that thrashing around wasn't going to do any good. She paid no attention.

Soon after, thankfully, the carriage stopped and the wall by our feet fell open. I blinked against the sudden light. Hands groped my feet, loosening the ropes. As soon as the Princess was freed, she began kicking, but two men grabbed her legs and dragged her out of the carriage. When they finished untying me, I kept still, and squirmed out on my own.

We were in a tiny clearing off a country lane. It appeared to be around five o'clock and my stomach confirmed that was about right. Our captors wore good clothes, not expensive suits but clothes that were well-made and clean. They all wore the same type of black bowler hat that matched the colour of

153

their vests, which John would have called waistcoats. They also wore scarves to cover their faces, which I was glad to see. If they didn't want us to see them, that meant they weren't planning on killing us. Or, the Princess, at least.

Two men held the Princess by her arms as she fought to get away. They seemed content to let her struggle and appeared to be waiting for her to give up.

My guard wasn't holding me, he was holding a gun, a rifle, like the one I'd seen in the exhibits, that held six shots. He motioned for me to turn around. With his free hand, he unbound me and took off the gag. When I turned back to face him, he put his finger up to where his mouth was underneath the scarf, and then pointed at his rifle. I nodded.

"I need …" I said, hoping he wouldn't shoot me but, by that time, not caring if he did.

He pointed to the edge of the clearing, and then to the rifle again. I didn't waste time nodding.

The other two were having a lot more trouble with the Princess. Eventually, they put a rope and harness on her. Only then did they untie her hands and take off her gag. She immediately started screaming. But the men just sat on the end of the wagon, one holding the rope attached to the Princess, who was lunging and struggling, trying to break free, while my guard, the Rifleman, looked on. Even though he had a scarf covering his face, I was pretty sure he was smiling.

It took a long time for the Princess's voice to go raw and for her to tire herself out. When she started flagging, they reeled her in. By that time, the Princess needed a comfort break, and let them know about it in no uncertain terms, along with her demand to be let go and to have a separate carriage because she wasn't going to travel in that tiny space with a commoner. They gave in to her demand for a comfort break, even lengthening the rope for her so she could have a bit of privacy. After that, they gave us each a drink of water and locked us back in the carriage.

# Chapter 28

## Charlie

"They're going to hang us," John said, panic in his voice.

"No, they're not." We were sitting on the floor again; the only place we could sit. "He's desperate to get his daughter back. He won't kill us if he thinks we have information."

"And when he finds out we really don't know anything about it?"

I looked up at the window and the fading light. "Well, he doesn't strike me as the type to murder two innocent boys for no reason."

John huffed and folded his arms over his chest. "You give the Royals too much credit."

I had to admit things couldn't look much gloomier. Then the door opened, and two guards came in. One carried a limp mattress stuffed with straw. He threw it into a corner and left without a word. The other had a wooden bucket, which he set in front of us. "You will sleep there," he said, pointing to the lumpy mattress, "and eat this." Then he left.

The meal was a thin stew, and since we'd been given no bowls or utensils, we had to scoop it out with our hands.

"Well, we know they're not going to hang us," I

said. "At least not any time soon."

"How," John asked, sucking gruel from his fingers.

"They would serve us a better last meal if they were."

John grimaced and scooped up more stew.

"Do you mean a Hangman's Meal? That's only if we could afford it."

"You mean they make you pay for it?"

"Of course."

The stew, which was awful, tasted even worse after that. I was hungry, though, so I ate it, and tried not to worry about Mitch, or the noose. When the door clanged open again, my heart jumped, but it was only the guard. This time, he carried a chair, and not a spindly, wooden one. It was large and sturdy, with cushioned arms and seat, and immediately followed by Albert, flanked by two guards. He was no longer wearing his red tunic, just satin pants, a crisp, white shirt, blue velvet jacket and thigh-high boots polished to a high shine.

"His Royal Highness Prince Albert of Saxe-Coburg and Gotha, Duke of Saxony," one of the guards announced. Albert sat in the chair.

"Stand in the presence of his Royal Highness," the other guard shouted at me. John was already standing.

The guards stood at attention on either side of the chair. Albert templed his fingers, rested his chin on them and stared at us, his face pale and drawn, his eyes filled with worry. He lifted one hand and, without glancing our way, waved it at the guards, who did an abrupt about face and left the cell. The door swung closed, the bolts clanged, and we were alone.

"My daughter has been kidnapped," he said.

My stomach lurched. What did that mean for

Mitch? Or us? I expected more, but he appeared to be waiting for us. Not knowing what to say, the silence stretched on until John finally broke it. "I am grieved to hear that, Your Royal Highness," he said, twisting his hat in his hands.

"I did not come for your condolences. I am here for answers." Albert gave him a look that I think was meant to intimidate, but there was such a weariness in him that it failed to impress. Still, John bowed his head and looked wretched.

"Bullying us isn't going to help you get them," I said. "We don't know any more than you do."

Now Albert's eyes did flash with anger. "How dare you—"

"Blah, blah, blah," I said, holding my hand up, opening and closing it as it if were talking. "You're not my king, I can talk to you any way I like."

John, and Albert, gasped.

"He's not the king," John hissed.

"Listen," I said, before Albert could jump in with more "don't talk to me like that" nonsense. "All I know is that my brother is missing, and I want to find him as much as you want to find your daughter. I can't tell you why his hat was found where your daughter was last seen. But now they're both gone. All I can tell you is, he didn't take her."

Albert shook his head sadly and stared at the floor. "These traitors, they have sent a letter. They want money. They say they will kill the Princess if they find out I have involved the Royal Guards or the police. I am taking a chance even coming to you. They are watching. Even this might get her killed, but I must do all I can to get her back."

I cleared my throat. "Can you pay them?"

It wasn't my place to ask, but it was the obvious question. I feared he would take offense, but the fight was drained from him; all he did was wave a hand in my direction. "Arrangements are being made. We have no way to contact these miscreants, but we will do as they ask."

"Then, maybe—"

"She is a child," he said, with surprising vehemence. "They are holding her in some gott verlassener ort. She cannot bear that. She should not have to suffer on account of us, they are tormenting her to get at me, and the Queen." Then he put his face in his hands and began sobbing. "My child, meine liebste, my dearest, my jewel."

"Jewel?"

Albert looked at me. I felt myself go white.

"You know something?"

"Um, I overheard … this had nothing to do with your daughter … or, well, I thought it didn't … men … I don't know who they were, I didn't see them … I swear, I, we, we didn't have anything to do with it …but—"

"Out with it," Albert shouted.

"Men, planning to steal a jewel. Me and John, we were protecting the jewels, but they must have been talking about your daughter. And Mitch must have figured it out."

Albert leapt from his chair, grabbed me by the arms and pushed me against the wall. "Why did you not tell me this?"

"It wasn't relevant," I sputtered.

"And if you knew they were planning to kidnap my daughter—"

"We didn't know!"

159

"—why didn't you alert someone?"

It was a fair question. But if I told him of Morgan's involvement, that would pit Morgan's word against mine, and then the police might get involved.

"It's complicated," I said.

"We are responsible for your great Exhibition," John said. "We are your loyal stewards. It is our duty to protect the Exhibition and all that is in it. We only did what we believed was expected of us."

Albert's grip eased. He stepped back and I stood, facing him.

"They didn't come for a jewel, like we thought," I said. "They came to kidnap your daughter. Mitch figured that out. He ran to save her. They must have taken him too."

Albert stalked back to his chair and sat heavily, glaring at me with renewed anger. "Perhaps, instead, they killed your brother and hid his body."

A lump of ice burst in my stomach. I was about to reply with, "And perhaps your daughter is with him," but I knew that would accomplish nothing except wound him further, which is what I wanted to do, and what I suspected he wanted me to do, because he, himself, was so wounded. Instead, I said, "We can't know that. The one thing I did hear was that no one was to be hurt. He said they were men of principle."

"Ha! Anarchists and traitors!"

"Well, yeah, but we have to believe that Mitch and your daughter are alive. We just need to find them."

The question "How?" hung in the room, unasked, because none of us knew the answer.

# Chapter 29

## Mitch

By the sway and bump of the carriage, I could tell we were travelling again. The Princess and I were crammed into the little box, bound and gagged, though not so brutally this time. The guy who tied us up—the one I thought of as The Jailer—only tied our hands, and the gags weren't as uncomfortably tight as they had been before.

The fresh air and exercise seemed to have done the Princess some good. It had drained the fight, and the desire to scream, out of her. All she did was weep softly and fall asleep.

I tried to sleep too, but couldn't. There were too many questions in my head. Who were these men? What did they want? What were they going to do with the Princess? To me? And what were John and Charlie and Mr. Merwyn doing? These questions and more kept going round and round in my head but, eventually, the boredom, and the gentle sway of the carriage, helped me drift off to sleep.

The next time we were let out of the carriage, it was dark. We were in a clearing, in a cluster of trees. The Rifleman had a fire going and was cooking something in a cast iron pan while the one I decided to call The Driver tended the horses. The Jailer led us to the fire and sat us down, then he pointed to the

Rifleman, who was squatting on the far side, cutting up whatever he had cooked in the big pan. He wasn't holding his rifle, but it was within easy reach.

"My friend there," the Jailer said, his voice muffled by the scarf covering his face, "can shoot your eye out at twenty paces, even in the dark. Now I'm going to untie you. You run and he'll pick you off before you get two paces. Understand?"

I nodded, but the Princess merely glared at him.

He untied me and removed my gag, then he started on the Princess.

"It she tries to run," he said, looking at me, "I'd advise you to stop her. We've no reason to keep you alive if we lose her."

I didn't think that would be any deterrent to the Princess, but it was an incentive for me to keep a close eye on her. To my relief, when he untied her hands, she didn't move. Then he took off her gag and she started screaming.

"Go ahead," he said, walking away with the ropes and gags, "scream your heart out. Ain't no one going to hear you."

She stopped after a few seconds, but that was probably because her voice was raw, not because of what he'd said.

For the first time since they'd taken us, I was relatively comfortable. The night was cool, but the fire was warm, and it felt good to stretch my cramped limbs. With the Princess finally quiet, all I could hear was the hum of insects, the crackle of the fire and the scrape of the Rifleman's knife against the iron pan. The smell of whatever was cooking wafted my way and I suddenly realize how hungry I was.

When the Driver joined them, they brought us

each a hunk of bread, a slab of burned meat and a tankard of water. The three of them sat on the far side of the fire from us, and I wondered why. Then I saw that, in order to eat, they'd needed to remove their masks. At that distance, and in the dim light, it was hard to make out their faces, and I didn't try. I wasn't going to give them any reason to shoot me. Instead, I concentrated on the food, my mouth watering as I waited for the Princess to take her share. But the Princess didn't eat. She sat with her arms folded and her bottom lip stuck out, glaring at the plate.

"I'm not eating that," she said.

"Well, you're not going to get anything else," I said. "So, it's this or nothing."

"Then I choose nothing," she said, kicking the dishes.

The water spilled, the bread and meat rolled into the fire and the metal plate landed in the coals, sending sparks flying. The men looked our way, but when they saw it was just another tantrum, they went back to their meal.

"Great," I said. "Now neither of us has anything to eat."

"Good," she said. "Because that's not food."

I sighed. "Look, you're not going to get French Cuisine out here. Take what you're given and be glad for it."

Her look hardened. "Don't presume to tell me—"

"I presume nothing," I said, raising my voice. "You've refused to eat, now you're going to go hungry. That's nothing to do with me. That's cause and effect."

Then she screamed again. "I want food, real food,

not swill they feed to pigs. If papa knew how I was being treated—"

"You should have eaten the swill," I shouted back. "I don't care if your father is king, you're still—"

"He's not king," she shrieked, then she launched herself at me.

It was such a surprise that I was on the ground and pinned before I knew what was happening. Fortunately, she was light. I pushed her off and rolled away, but she came right back, punching and kicking and flailing her arms while the men looked on and laughed. It was difficult to fight back without hurting her. I tried to grab her hands, and when I did, she bit me on the arm. That made me mad. I threw her down, sat on her and pinned her to the ground. She kicked her feet, thrashed her head and snarled.

I bent my head low. "You've got to stop this, Princess. For your own—"

Then she head-butted me.

That did it. I let go of one of her arms long enough to slap her across the face, then I pinned her down again. She stopped screaming and looked at me with wide, angry eyes. "Why you … you …"

"No, you," I said. "You've got to stop this. We need to be calm, and rational. We've got to think, and work together if we're going to get out of this."

"Papa will come for me," she hissed, "and he'll hang you."

"That may be, but he isn't doing such a good job so far. And if we can escape before he has to negotiate with these people, all the better."

"Why would papa negotiate?" she asked, her voice quiet at last.

"You've been kidnapped, you dolt. They'll want

164

money, and if your father is as devoted to you as you think, he'll pay them. Although, if you keep acting this way, it might be them that pays your father to take you off their hands."

She stopped struggling, but I still didn't trust her enough to let her go.

"Oh, poor Papa, he'll be so worried, and angry, and … oh, what am I going to do?"

"Keep your voice down, for one," I said. "Behave yourself and give me time to think."

"You're a commoner, you don't tell me—"

"Right now, I do. You're a prisoner, just like me. And I have more experience with this than you do, so shut up, stop your antics and let me try to figure something out."

She glared at me but said nothing.

"That's enough you love-birds," one of the men shouted. "Cut it short and get back to the fire."

"I need to let you up now," I said. "Do I have your word you won't attack me, or scream, or run around being petulant?"

"Yes."

"Your word?"

"You have my word. Now let me up."

I got off her and backed away, wary, but all she did was stand, brush herself off and sit by the fire. I sat next to her.

After a few minutes of silence, she sighed. "I wish now that I hadn't thrown my food and water away. I'm thirsty, and hungry, and those miscreants are probably laughing at me."

"Maybe," I said, "but let me try something. And don't interfere."

I stood up. The Rifleman reached for the gun, but

when he saw I wasn't running, he relaxed. "Sirs," I said, "the Princess regrets her actions. May she have some water, and food? It isn't good for her to be so thirsty and hungry. She may get sick. That wouldn't be good for any of us."

The Jailer laughed, but the Rifleman nodded and put on his mask. Carrying the rifle, he left the campfire and went to the wagon, returning with some raw meat. Then he knelt at the dying fire and began cooking over the glowing coals. It might have been my imagination, but he seemed to be taking more care. What I smelled was cooked, not burnt, meat. The Driver looked on impassively, but the Jailer scowled.

"You're not going to serve them our victuals, are you?"

"I'll do as I see fit," the Rifleman said without looking up, "and you'll have nought to say about it. Now fetch the plate and cup."

The Jailer glared at the back of the Rifleman's head but said nothing. Then he got up and started toward us.

"Mask," the Rifleman shouted.

The Jailer pulled a handkerchief from his vest pocket and tied it around his face, but not before I saw his stubbled face and bushy moustache. He kicked the plate and metal cup out of the fire, sending a shower of sparks over us and making the Princess scoot back in alarm. A few embers landed on the ruffles and lace of her dress, and she batted at them furiously until I was able to brush them away with my foot.

The Rifleman cleaned the plate and cup with a rag, and cut up the meat, which looked tender and juicy.

Still wearing his mask, he brought bread, water and the meat, along with a metal fork, to the Princess.

As he placed it on the ground in front of her, she managed to not glare at him. As he walked away, I poked her with an elbow.

"Thank him," I said.

"I will not!"

I thought she had a point, so I didn't push it.

The Princess guzzled the water, stuffed hunks of bread into her mouth and shovelled up the meat. I didn't remark on her table manners, or that she had left none for me; I was just glad she had seen reason.

An hour later, the Jailer took the Princess to the wagon. He threw two blankets into the compartment, locked her in, then came to me carrying another blanket.

"You'll sleep here," he said, throwing it at me.

The Driver built the fire back up and the three of them sat on the far side, their masks off, sharing a bottle and talking about things men usually talk about when they're drinking, which is nothing in particular, but making it sound important. I wrapped in the blanket and laid still, hoping they would think I was asleep and start talking about what they were up to. But they were too smart for that. Instead, they passed the bottle back and forth and talked in low voices. The bottle went from the Rifleman to the Jailer to the Driver, then back again, which meant the Jailer was taking two gulps for each of theirs. And he was gulping, unlike the Rifleman, who was taking sips and looking at the Jailer with increasing disapproval.

After a while, when I was really starting to fall asleep, the Rifleman didn't pass the bottle back to the Jailer.

"That's enough," he said, when the Jailer reached for it. "You'll need to stand guard, and you'll be lucky to sleep this off before your turn. Now you two get to the wagon. You can sleep there. I'll take the first watch."

Grumbling, the Jailer rose and followed the Driver to the wagon.

"You snore again tonight," the Driver said, "I'm rolling you off the edge."

"Do that," the Jailer said, his voice trailing into the darkness, "and you'll answer for it."

The Rifleman put the bottle aside, laid the rifle across his lap and sat, watching. I pulled the blanket tighter around me and fell asleep.

Hours later I woke. It was still dark, but dawn was not far off. I kept still, hoping to fall back asleep. Then I saw the Jailer was sitting close by—close enough that I could clearly see his face—holding the rifle and staring at me.

"Think you're clever, do ya, boy?"

I realized he was talking to me. "No," I said.

"I heard you plotting with that wildcat. You think you can outsmart us. Get away."

"No," I said again. "We're going to wait for the ransom to be paid."

I wondered why we were having a conversation, then I saw him pick up a bottle from behind him and take a drink.

"Ransom," he said, his voice slurred. "That's a diversion. You're nothing but a decoy."

He was drunk, and he had a rifle. I needed to be careful.

"I'm sure you'll get your money," I said. "Her father is—"

"Her father is dead," he shouted. "And her mother"

I waited to see if he had woken anyone, but no one came.

"Holding your little friend, there," he said, waving a hand toward the wagon, "is so they will give the signal. Not so they will pay any money. Do you think we're stupid enough to try to get money out of them? Do you, boy?"

He punctuated his statement by pointing the rifle at me. I sucked in an involuntary breath.

"No, sir, I don't."

"There's a chair," he said, ignoring me. "When the Exhibition opens, she'll be there, with the foreigner." I assumed by this he meant Albert and Queen Victoria. "And she's to sit in it if they've paid the money, or just walk past it if they have not." Then he laughed, and I wished he'd put the rifle down before he accidentally pulled the trigger. "But the joke's on them. The Boss doesn't care about money, only that he gets a clear shot, and that's what the chair is for."

That meant we didn't have a lot of time to get away, if indeed we could. But it also made me wonder about the rest of their plans.

"What about us?"

To my relief, he lowered the rifle.

"The Boss, he's got a soft heart. He thinks we should let you go after he's done his duty." Then he pointed the rifle at me again. "But I think, once I'm left alone with you, you will both be shot trying to escape."

He started shaking with laughter again, but he laid the rifle down and took another swig from his bottle. I closed my eyes and pretended to sleep. We needed to get away, and we needed to do it soon. And, above all, I needed to keep what I had just learned from the Princess.

## Chapter 30
### Wednesday, 30 April 1851

## Charlie

Morning came, and I woke, stiff and sore from sleeping on the thin mattress, and with a stuffy head from smelling the mouldy hay all night. A guard brought us a bucket of something grey and soupy that smell vaguely like oatmeal, and we ate it in silence, with no speculation about it being a Hangman's Meal.

After breakfast, I pounded on the door to ask the guard if I could be let out to use the bathroom. When no one came, I used the bucket our breakfast soup had been in, hoping they wouldn't serve it to us for lunch.

An hour later, the door opened again. I expected it to be Albert, with more threats, but it was a couple of the guards bringing furniture. They carried in two wooden chairs and a small table, then a bed, with a thicker mattress, and blankets. One of them began sweeping out the straw and another—after looking into the bucket and grimacing—took our breakfast dishes away. Me and John stood in a corner, out of the way, as they arranged our now-crowded prison cell. Before they left, they put a lamp on the table, and even lit it. Then they left, locking the door behind them.

We sat on the bed, enjoying the softness of the

171

mattress after so many hours on the floor, and wondering aloud what it all meant. Soon after, the guards returned with another meal. A real meal of hot stew, cooked beef, potatoes and wine that they arranged on the table, complete with bowls and cutlery. Wooden cutlery, I noticed. When we were alone again, we sat at the table and cautiously began to eat. Neither of us wanted to say aloud what I was sure we were both thinking: this really did look like a Hangman's Meal.

Half an hour later, the door opened, and my heart skipped a beat, expecting to see a guard with a hangman's noose. But it was only Albert, looking haggard and dressed in plain pants and a loose shirt that at one time might have been white. His hair was dishevelled, his eyes bloodshot. We stood, and since his chair hadn't been carried in for him, we offered him one of ours. He waved it away and stood erect, his hands behind his back. "The traitors have sent word. They wish our answer tomorrow noon."

"And what are you going to tell them."

He sighed, so long and deep that his head drooped and his shoulders slumped. "As a father, I have no choice. I would give in to their demands. I want my daughter back."

"Well," I said, "that's not ideal, but if all it's going to cost you is money—"

He raised his head. "You do not understand. As a father, I have no choice, but as Monarch, my wife has no choice either. Daughter, or not, we do not negotiate with traitors. If petty criminals can bend the Royal family of Great Britain to their will, where would it end?"

The silence lengthened and grew heavy. Was he

not going to pay? Was he going to let them kill his daughter? And what about Mitch? And then another question came to me. "Why are you telling us this?"

"Because your brother was mentioned in their communication."

"What? Is he okay? Are they going to let him go? Where did they take him? Why did they take him?"

I waited. At last, Albert spoke. "They believe him to be a Royal companion. So long as they believe he is someone of value to our household, he will be safe. I wanted you to know that. He is no longer considered a criminal. Nor are the two of you."

"So, we can go?"

"No."

"But—"

"This dreadful episode must be handled with the utmost secrecy. Outside of a few soldiers and advisers loyal to the crown, no one knows of the kidnapping. Only you, myself and my wife. And the traitors."

For the first time I noticed he had no guards with him.

"So, what are you going to do? Keep us here? Forever?"

"It will be made known that the Princess Royal was taken suddenly ill," Albert said, gazing at a point just above my head. "Her death will be announced in two weeks. The truth will remain safe within the Palace circle."

When he said nothing further, I added. "As long as we stay locked up here."

Beside me, John let out a groan.

Albert cleared his throat. "You will be afforded all the necessary comforts."

"But … but …"

173

"We won't tell anyone," John said, his voice so high it squeaked. "Honest."

"If the choice was mine, it would be different. This is what our advisers proposed, and my wife, the Queen, our sovereign, has commanded, and I—"

"Your wife's a monster!"

John slapped a hand over his mouth, attempting to stifle a horrified gasp.

"She's letting them kill her daughter," I continued. "And my brother. You can't let this happen, you can't."

Albert looked at me, his eyes moist. "Emotions," he said softly. "I'm afraid they are a luxury those who rule cannot afford. And, in this case, I am glad to not be a Ruler, for I could not make such a decision. My wife, the Queen, is stronger than I. She knows her duty."

"But you have to do something, anything."

Albert shook his head. "There is nothing to be done. I just wanted you to know, after what you've been through, that you are no longer considered criminals. I regret that you have been caught up in this. And I regret that your brother gave his life attempting to save my daughter. It is because of his heroics that you are to be treated well."

"He's not dead yet. There's still time."

But Albert turned away. "There's nothing to be done," he said, walking toward the door. "My daughter will die, and this will be your home until you die."

"There's always something that can be done," I shouted as he called the guard. "There's always something!" He stepped into the corridor. The door slammed behind him. I ran to it and pressed my face

174

to the metal grill, pounding my fists on the unyielding oak.

"There's always something," I shouted, as he descended the circular stairs. "There's always something."

# Chapter 31

## Mitch

In the morning, the Rifleman left, taking a horse and the rifle with him. This gave me hope, because it left only the Jailer and the Driver, who were both unarmed, guarding us. But then I discovered they had another six-shooter rifle stashed in the wagon, and my hopes sank. The only good thing was that the Jailer was asleep, snoring next to the fire. I hoped he might stay that way for a while but, just before he left, the Rifleman kicked him.

"Get moving," he said. "We've a schedule to keep to. And if I catch you drunk again, it'll be the last time."

The Rifleman didn't stay for an answer. But the Jailer rolled over and mumbled, "Yes, Boss."

The Driver cooked up something that resembled pancakes, which I ate with more enthusiasm than the Princess, or the Jailer. But then, she'd had dinner, and I hadn't spent the night drinking.

After breakfast, we were locked in the wagon again, but without being bound and gagged.

Oddly, lying next to the Princess, without being tied up, was awkward. I felt like I should move away from her but, of course, there was no place to go, so we had to lay uncomfortably close, trying to ignore each other.

After an hour or two of silence, the Princess asked, "Why haven't they tied us up?" Her voice rasped. I suspected her throat was raw.

"I guess they're not worried about you screaming," I said. "I think we're not close enough to any people for that to be a problem anymore."

"Where do you think we are."

I thought for a moment. "We seem to be travelling south. This wagon is very slow, so we can't have gone far. Thirty miles, maybe."

"But where are we going?"

"I wish I knew. We just need to be ready for when we do get there."

The Princess snorted. "Ready? How are we supposed to do that?"

"By keeping our strength up—and that means eating and drinking what they give us—resting, and co-operating as much as possible. We don't want to be problem prisoners. The easier we make it for them, the more likely it is they'll drop their guard, and we need to be ready when they do."

"You sound like you've done this before."

I thought back to our other adventures, trying—and failing—to recall one where we hadn't been held prisoner.

We stopped twice for comfort breaks and each time I searched the leaden skies for the sun, hoping it could help me figure out the time of day or our direction of travel. It never appeared, but still, it felt like we were going south. I wasn't sure why I thought this, until our second time out of the wagon, when I could see a bit of the landscape and an abandoned shed in a field at the side of the road. The rolling hills reminded me of Sussex, the ground was chalky, and the tumbled-down walls of the derelict shed were made of flint. So, we were, it seemed, heading south. Though, having congratulated myself for figuring this out, I had to admit it didn't give us much of an advantage.

Back in the cramped carriage, we struggled to get comfortable. The Princess was cranky, the air stale and I felt like banging my head against the wall to knock myself out. Instead, I just laid next to her, waiting. Then, after what seemed like ages, the wagon stopped.

After they extracted the Princess, I squirmed into the daylight and stood on wobbling legs. The Driver—wearing a mask—held the Princess by an arm but, exhausted and disoriented, she wasn't struggling. The Jailer, holding the rifle, stood behind me. Like the Driver, he was wearing a mask, but I had not forgotten that he had let me see his face clearly the night before. I took a quick look around, hoping to find an advantage.

We appeared to be in a farmyard. A ramshackle house sat some distance away, and there was a dilapidated barn, and a few smaller out-buildings, in the other direction. The yard itself was dry, the ground hard packed and scattered with rusting pieces of farm equipment. The lack of wagon-wheel ruts and the abundance of weeds told me it was deserted. This was where they were going to keep us.

The farm was in a shallow valley surrounded by stunning scenery. On a hill, in the distance, was a windmill, with its sails rotating slowly in the breeze. It seemed so out of place that I couldn't stop staring at it. The rifle barrel nudged me in the back and the Jailer pointed to a nearby building—a storage shed with thick walls, a high, pitched roof and a heavy wooden door that stood open. I sighed and walked toward it while the Driver dragged the Princess, who started screaming again.

They pushed the Princess in first. She tripped and fell, and then I tripped on the Princess, falling on top of her.

She pushed me off with surprising force. "How dare you!" She jumped up and ran to the door, already closed and bolted. "Let me out! I demand to be released. I am a princess, you can't do this to me."

"Princess," I said, "please stop. You're not helping."

But she kept on.

"Princess," I said, louder. "Princess Victoria."

"I will not be treated this way. Papa will make you pay for this—"

"Vicky, cut it out!"

The silenced that followed was so absolute I could hear the rumble of a train in the distance. She turned and fixed me with a malevolent gaze. "You will not address me in that manner," she said through clenched teeth. "I am Her Royal Highness, Victoria, The Princess Royal—"

"Not in here you're not. You're just another prisoner, and you're acting like a spoiled child—"

"I am not a child. I am eleven years old."

"I don't care if you're fifty-seven. Shut up, sit down and help me think of a way to get out of here."

"My Papa will rescue us."

"So you keep saying, but we're still here."

That put an end to it. She opened her mouth to say more, then closed it. Her eyes moved away from me to the thick walls, the high, narrow windows, and the single pile of straw covered in blankets that lay in one corner. Her eyes widened and her lip began to tremble, then she covered her face in her hands and started crying. "Why didn't they bring us to the house? Why can't they put us in someplace more salubrious? I can't stay here. I can't. We're never going to get out of here."

She leaned back against the door and slid to the floor, her dress and petticoats rumpled up around her. She ignored them and continued to sob. I took a few, hesitant steps toward her. Should I try to comfort her? That might start her screaming again, although that would have been an improvement. "Look, Princess," I said, "we'll think of something." But that only made her cry harder. I sat down next to her, my back against the door. "I've been in situations like this before, and I got out."

She made a sound like "Pwaaahhh!"

"No, really. Me, my brother, and a girl, a princess, like you."

"You're making this up."

"I'm not, I swear. We were in a room, just like this, and she helped us escape."

Her sobbing eased a little. "The Princess?"

"Yes, she was very brave, and noble. She helped us even though she was sick, dying, and couldn't come with us."

"You left her behind?"

"No, we couldn't do that. We took her with us. We all escaped."

"Did she die?"

"No, she lived. And then she saved our lives. I told you, she was noble, and brave."

Her sobs petered out. Her hands and face were

wet and slimy. "Not like me, then." She covered her face again, muffling a sound that was somewhere between a sob and a laugh, spraying more snot into her hands. She looked around for something to wipe them on. I pulled up the bottom of my shirt and offered it to her. This time, she did laugh.

"Well, it's all I have," I said.

In the end, she pulled off one of the many ribbons on her dress and used that as a handkerchief. Then she moved to the pile of straw and sat on that for what little comfort it gave, and I took a good look around the room. I didn't want to admit that she might be right, but I was coming to that conclusion. It was easy to see why they hadn't put us in the house. There were probably a dozen ways to escape from any room. They'd have to keep a very close eye on us. Here, there was no way out. They could just lock us in and forget us. And, after the conversation with the Jailer, I was just as glad for it.

The door had been reinforced with new hinges, and the wood, though dry and weathered, was sturdy. The windows weren't really windows at all but more like slits for ventilation, and they were too high to get to anyway.

"Papa will get us out," the Princess said when she saw me becoming frustrated. "There's no way we can escape."

I sat down against the wall, hugging my knees and glaring at the door.

"We can't rely on that," I said. "There's no way he can find us."

"And there's no way you're going to get us out."

Her attitude really annoyed me, but before I could say anything the door opened, and the Jailer entered. I was pleased to see he was unarmed. He carried a bucket in one hand, a leather pouch in the other and had a blanket slung over his shoulder. He wore a scarf over his face, but that didn't ease my discomfort.

"Food," he said. "And an extra blanket for the unexpected guest."

He plopped the bucket down next to the Princess, slopping water onto the dirt floor, and dropped the blanket next to it. Then he upended the pouch and dumped bread, cheese and two wooden cups onto the blanket.

"Enjoy your stay," he said, turning to leave.

"Wait," the Princess called. "What about our … comfort?"

He turned to face us. I could tell by his eyes that he was amused. "Your comfort?" he pointed to the water bucket. "Empty that, then fill it." He apparently thought that was hugely funny because he bent over laughing.

The Princess reddened. "You surely cannot expect me to—"

"Suit yourself," he said, still chuckling as he walked out the door. It banged shut behind him, and a bolt snapped into place.

While the Princess sulked, I divided up the food, folded the blanket and sat on it. I took my time doing it, hoping she would calm down, but when I offered her a cup of water, she knocked it out of my hand.

"I'm not eating or drinking anything until we get out of here," she said. "This is beastly, absolutely beastly and I will not put up with it."

I thought about arguing with her but decided it would be pointless. I left food and water next to her—but not close enough where she could kick it—

182

and sat against the far wall, facing her while I ate. When I finished, we just sat, glaring at each other while the light grew dimmer.

"Listen," I said. "We will get out of here. Like you said, your father will pay the ransom, they'll let us go, you'll get clean clothes, good food, a comfortable bed, but you've got to endure this first and that will be easier to do if you are not hungry and tired." I felt bad lying to her, but I thought it best to give her some hope. "I've eaten, and now I'm going to sleep. I suggest you do the same."

I laid on the hard ground, covered myself with the blanket and tried to sleep. As the light dimmed, the Princess finally ate and drank. Then she, too, laid down to sleep. But as the darkness became absolute, I heard her tossing and turning and grumbling.

"I'm cold," she said.

I sighed. "So am I."

"But I'm really cold," she said, on the verge of sobbing, "I'm shivering, and I'm scared."

I sighed again and felt my way toward her. When I found her bed, I laid my blanket over her. She was shivering badly, and her teeth chattered. I remembered how we had huddled together for warmth while in the field with Harold's army, but I doubted the Princess would allow that. Still, I couldn't just leave her, so I laid down next to her, expecting her to scream any second. Instead, she pressed against me and, after a while, her shaking eased, and then she fell asleep.

I laid awake for a while, thinking about Charlie, John and Mr. Merwyn, and how worried they would be. Were they looking for me? Did they know where I was, or who I was with? I put it out of my mind. The

Princess was right, there was nothing I could do. I would just have to wait and hope things looked better in the morning.

They didn't.

# Chapter 32
**Thursday, 1 May 1851**

# Charlie

I opened my eyes. It was still dark in the cell, but I could see grey dawn through the arched and barred window. Me and John were clothed, covered in as many blankets as we could find and lying close in the centre of the bed to keep off the damp chill of the cell. And it was a cell, a prison. It was not our home, it never would be our home, and I wasn't going to spend another day there if I could help it.

Me and John had talked late into the night, trying to figure out a plan, hoping we could think of something, anything, to get us out of the cell. But, of course, we failed.

When we had finally fallen into bed, sleep wouldn't come. Not for me, anyway. John drifted right off, but I kept thinking there had to be something we could do. No answers came, though, and the harder I pounded my head against that mental wall, the stronger it became. I didn't know where they were. That was the only thing that might save them, the one thing I needed to know. And I had no way of finding out.

But as I opened my eyes, the answer came to me.

I jumped out of bed and ran to the door. "Guard," I shouted, pounding my fists on the door.

Behind me, John groaned. "What are you doing? We agreed there was nothing we could do."

"No," I said, running back to the bed. "I've figured it out, I know how to find out where they are. We need to tell Albert."

John pushed the covers away and sat up, suddenly awake. "Really? Are you sure?"

"Well, I think so," I said, running back to the door. "It's a chance, anyway." I started pounding again. "Guard, I need to speak to the King."

Behind me, John groaned. "He's not the King."

A horse voice echoed down the stone corridor. "Shut yer gob!"

I put my face up to the grill. "I need to see the … Queen's husband. Albert. I need to see him, now."

"G'wan, you daft bugger! I'm no disturbing His Majesty. Do I look as daft as you?"

"Listen," I said. "This is no joke. Your future, your life, may depend on this."

Now the voice came closer. "Bloody 'el, I've better things to do with my time than play nursemaid to you whelps. Shoulda hung ya when I had the chance."

"Something terrible is going to happen today," I said. "Albert does not want it to happen. I know how to stop it. He must be told. Now."

The guard stopped in front of me, his uniform rumpled, his hair unkempt. "Then you shoulda' told him when he was here."

"That's just it," I said. "He wanted me to help him. He wanted it desperately, and I wanted to help him too. But I didn't have the information he needed. Or, I didn't know I had it. I do now, I remember what it is I need to tell him. I must see him now or it will be too late."

"You expect me to disturb His Majesty—"

"He will be grateful," I said, "very grateful."

The guard rubbed his chin. "In a monetary way, do you think?"

"I don't know. But I do know, for a fact, that if you do not tell him, he will be very, very ungrateful."

The man continued stroking his chin.

"And if you send word, I won't tell Albert you were sleeping on duty."

He suddenly became convinced. "All right. I'll do it, but it will be on your head."

"Swiftly," I said. "Use your fastest horse."

"Don't bloody push me," he growled, ambling away.

But his footsteps, as soon as he was out of my sight, quickened.

"Do you think he'll really summon the prince?" John asked, appearing beside me.

"We'll know soon enough," I said, "and we'll need to move fast once he gets here."

"Can't you simply tell him what you know?"

I left the door and sat in one of the chairs. "I still don't know anything. I just think I know a way to find out what I need to know. And to do that, I have to convince Albert to let us out of here."

John slumped into the other chair. "He's never going to agree to that."

"And we need to find Mr. Merwyn."

John covered his face with his hands. "I thought you had a good idea. That could take—"

"I think I know how to find him, though," I said. "And I think, when we get to where we're going, he'll be there."

# Chapter 33

## Mitch

I woke at first light and slipped carefully from under the blankets, trying to keep as much of the cold away from the Princess as I could. To keep warm, I paced the room, hugging myself.

In the dim light, I inspected every inch of the room. There was dirt, rocks, straw, the Princess, myself, and a heavy wooden door, the same as the night before, and none of those things would help us escape.

I shoved my hands into my pockets to thaw my fingers and felt metal, warmed by my body heat. The glass cutter, still in my pocket. Another item to add to the list. But would it make a difference?

I paced the room again. Thinking hard. Forgetting the Princess, I kicked at one of the rocks. It careened off the wall with a sharp clack, emitting a few sparks. The Princess sat up with a start. "What was that? Are they shooting?"

"No," I said. "It was just me. I'm sorry I woke you."

She sat against the wall, pulling the blankets around her. "No bother, though I was having such a peaceful dream. Are you still trying to figure a way out of here?"

I nodded. "Yes, but I'm having no better luck than

I was last night."

The Princess sighed. "You should give up. Papa will get us out."

I nodded, but kept pacing, and thinking.

A few minutes later, I heard the sound of a door creaking open. Then the neighing of horses and the groan of the wagon.

"Are they moving us?" the Princess asked.

I sat by the door, listening.

There were the usual sounds of horses being hitched. Then someone climbed into the wagon's seat. The reins snapped and the clip-clop of hooves passed close to the door, then faded. The Driver was leaving. I did some quick calculations in my head. Judging from the speed we had been moving, we were about forty miles from where we had started in London. The wagon, with two horses and nobody but the driver in it, could do about ten miles an hour. If it was five, or even six, in the morning, he'd be in London well before noon, which was when the opening ceremony was. The Rifleman was probably already there, getting ready to shoot the King and Queen, even though Albert wasn't the King.

And that left only the Jailer to watch over us. And he would have the rifle.

I took a breath, trying to keep myself calm.

"No," I said. "That was just them taking the wagon."

"They're abandoning us," she said.

If only, I thought. The only hope we had was if the Jailer had spent the night drinking again. With the Rifleman gone, that was a good bet, but he'd still wake up sooner or later, and we needed to be gone when he did.

189

"We're never going to get out of here," she said, her voice on the edge of tears, again.

I moved away from the door and took a splinter out of my cheek. The wood was dry as tinder, and rough, and it made me think of the door to the room we had escaped from with Kayla. Then it clicked.

"Yes, we will," I said.

"Will what?" She asked.

"Get out of here."

"How," she said, her voice mocking, though her eyes were full of hope.

"We're going to burn our way out."

# Chapter 34

## Charlie

We waited a long time, so long I was afraid the guard had lied and was back at his post enjoying a snooze, or that the message had reached Albert and he had ignored it. We waited in silence, watching the drizzling dawn appear, hoping I was right, and that we weren't too late.

Then footsteps echoed in the hall, hurrying our way. The bolt slid back, the door opened, and Albert stepped through, dressed in his normal clothes, if you think thigh-high boots, red pants and a blue, high-collared jacket with gold buttons is normal. In the flickering candlelight, his eyes glowed with hope, and suspicion.

"You lied," he said. "I asked for information, and you lied."

I folded my arms across my chest and shook my head. "I didn't lie. If I had known anything, don't you think I would have told you, if only to save my brother?"

"But you do know."

"I don't. Not yet. But I think I know a way to find out."

Albert's eyes narrowed. The hope had dimmed, all I saw was suspicion. "How?"

"Take us to the Talisman."

# Chapter 35

## Mitch

"How are we supposed to do that?" the Princess asked. "We don't have anything to start a fire with, and we don't have anything to burn."

I walked toward the door, pulling the glass cutter from my pocket, not bothering to turn around to address Her Highness. "You're wrong. We have both."

I heard a sharp intake of breath. She said nothing, but I could practically feel her glaring at me. I jammed the end of the glass cutter into a crack near one of the hinges and pulled, using all my weight. It bent, then snapped, sending me tumbling to the ground. In my hand I held half of the glass cutter, the exposed metal shining dimly in the half-light. The edge was ragged but sharp. It wouldn't stay sharp long, but it would do.

At the base of the door, where the wood was weakened with dry rot. I used the broken cutter like a chisel, sheering off bits of wood and gouging deep grooves lined with curled shavings and splinters.

"You're not going to be able to cut through the door with that," the Princess said. "It would take days."

"I just need to scuff it up," I said. "It will provide a bit of wood for the fire and make it easier for the door to burn.

When the door was sufficiently prepared, and I had gathered a small pile of wood shavings, I went to the wall, running my hands over the stones until I found one of the right type that would be easy to remove. The ancient cement was still strong, and the cutter was a poor tool, but I kept at it, making a tiny dent with each stroke. My hands were raw and my arms felt like jelly by the time the stone became loose enough to pull out of the wall.

When it finally tumbled free, I sat back, sweating and breathing hard. I rested, waiting, and outside heard a sound that left me cold.

It was raining.

# Chapter 36

## Charlie

Albert hesitated. "I do not know what you are asking."

"There is an exhibit in the Exhibition Hall, displaying artifacts held by the Royal Family. In it, there is a black stone called the Talisman. We need to go to it."

Albert shook his head. "You try to trick me. I let you out, you run."

I jumped out of my seat. "And let my brother die? No, I need to see the Talisman."

"That trinket is just an old stone. You cannot—"

"That trinket has the power to save your daughter's life," I said, striding toward him.

Albert stood his ground, his fists on his hips. "Now you sound like my wife. All these fairy tales of this Talisman, how it was given to the sovereign Elizabeth by ancient knights, Guardians, who told her she must—"

"Use it wisely," I said.

Albert scowled at me. "How do you, a common boy, know of this?"

"I was there," I said. "I am one of the Knights, one of the Guardians. It was us, my brother and me, who gave the Talisman to Queen Elizabeth."

Albert laughed. "Now I know you are simply

insane." He pointed at John. "Is he three-hundred years old, as well?"

I realized I might be making a terrible mistake, but I did my best to hide it. "No," I said, keeping my gaze on Albert, "and neither am I. I don't expect you to understand."

"But you expect me to believe you."

That had me stumped. There was nothing I could do or say to prove I wasn't lying. Then I thought of something, a slim chance, but it might work.

"The Talisman is guarded by a Druid Priest," I said. "He is not three hundred years old; he is thousands of years old. If you take us to the Talisman, you will find him there, and you will know I am not lying."

Albert shook his head and turned to go. "This is simply a desperate ploy to escape. I have no time for this."

"It's a desperate ploy to save my brother," I shouted after him. "To save your daughter, the Princess, your jewel. Don't you owe her this?"

Albert stopped, his hand on the door.

"After they kill Princess Victoria," I continued. "You will be haunted by this for the rest of your life. Yes, it's crazy, and, yes, it may come to nothing, but it's a chance, and if you don't take it, you will wake every morning to a world without Princess Victoria and the knowledge that you didn't do everything you could to try to save her."

I expected him to become angry, maybe even come after me, but he just stood there in the half-open doorway, his hand resting on the iron bolt. Then his head slumped, and his shoulders began to shake. "Come with me," he said.

195

We followed him, past the astonished guard, our own heads bowed. I had won, but I didn't feel good about it.

# Chapter 37

## Mitch

It took a while to crack the flint rock in half, but after half a dozen smacks against the wall it finally split in two, leaving me with a shiny, flat surface to work with. I made dozens of sparks while breaking it, but I had less luck striking the cutter on the stone. I tried to do it the way Kayla had, but nothing happened.

"I don't know what you think you're doing, but it isn't going to work."

I sighed and looked at the Princess, still sitting against the wall wrapped in the blankets. "I just need to get the angle right," I said. I struck the rock with more determination and got a spark. "There," I said. "It does work."

The Princess rolled her eyes. "It's raining, dummkopf. You can't start a fire in the rain."

She'd been calling me 'dummkopf' since I'd told her she was wrong. I think it was her way of telling me she was smarter than I was.

"It isn't raining that hard," I said, "and if I can get a good enough fire going, it will dry the outside of the door. I know that, and I'm a dummkopf."

I struck the flint again and got more sparks. I tried to direct them onto the pile of threads and fluff I had gathered but most of them missed, and the few that did land glowed briefly and went out.

Behind me, the Princess snorted. "You are a dummkopf, and I'm a princess, and you'll never get a fire going like that. Dummkopf."

I turned around. She was still sitting on the straw, wrapped in the blankets, her eyes puffy, her hair lopsided and tangled. I could see she expected me to start shouting at her, and the truth is, I felt like doing just that. But, instead, I forced myself to remain calm and looked directly into her eyes.

"You're no princess," I said. "A princess is brave, and resourceful, and noble. A princess never gives up, she doesn't wallow in self-pity. Kayla never gave up. If she had, I wouldn't be here. Kayla was a princess. You're just … Vicky."

I turned back to the pile of threads and hit the flint. Sparks flew, glowed, and died.

Behind me, the Princess started crying again, and outside, the rain came down harder.

# Chapter 38

## Charlie

It was nearly five o'clock when we reached the Crystal Palace. It was just getting light, and rain was falling but the whole site was swarming with people. It was mostly workmen, making final arrangements for the opening ceremonies, but members of the public were there too, crowding around the entrance, hoping to get a place inside when the doors opened.

Albert told the driver to take us to a side entrance and the carriage clattered, unnoticed, past the crowd, carrying me and John and the man everyone was clamouring to see. At the far end, we jumped from the carriage and ran to the door. Albert identified himself to the men guarding it, telling them he was there on a surprise, but secret, inspection and that got us inside.

The great entrance hall may have been bustling, but the edges of the Palace remained dark and deserted. We moved along the hallway at a trot, scanning around to make sure we weren't being watched. Soon, we arrived at the exhibit where the Talisman was on display in its glass case. We stopped in front of it and looked around. We were alone, and I suddenly realized I didn't have any idea about what to do.

"Here is your Talisman, young man," Albert said.

"Now tell me where Princess Victoria is."

I stared at the glass case. "I need to hold it," I said. "It … I've never had it show me anything unless it was in my hands."

"Just as I thought," Albert said. "A thief, as well. You bring me here by giving me false hope and fancy stories, and now you want me to break open this case so you can steal the artifact."

"No, that's not true," I said. And before I could say anything else, Albert grabbed me and John.

"You won't be escaping," he said, dragging us away. "And you won't be fooling me again. It's back to the Tower for you."

"If I can just touch it," I said.

Albert shook his head. "Such a fool, such a fool."

I didn't know if he meant me or himself, but I heard the regret, and the sadness, in his voice.

"We've come this far," I said, struggling against him. "Just open the case. Let me hold the Talisman. If that doesn't work, you can lock us up and throw away the key."

"That won't be necessary."

I thought Albert had said it, but he stopped, stood straight and looked around, his eyes alert. Then Mr. Merwyn stepped out of the shadows, though I only knew it was Mr. Merwyn because I knew who he was. To Albert, and John, he must have looked frightening: a ghost-like figure, dressed in a white robe that brushed the floorboards, holding a gnarled, wooden staff in his hand. Albert tensed, ready to fight. John gasped.

"I'll call the guards," Albert said.

Mr. Merwyn moved forward, seeming to glide over the floor. "That won't be necessary either," he said. "I have come to save your daughter, and you."

Albert blanched. "What do you know of my daughter? You are the kidnapper. This is all part of your diabolical plot. Guards!"

Mr. Merwyn came closer. Albert began to shake, but with fear or rage I couldn't tell. He remained frozen to the spot, watching the bearded apparition glide toward him.

Mr. Merwyn laid a hand on his shoulder. "I assure you, that is not the case," he said, his voice quiet, soothing. "Let the boys go. Let Charlie look into the Talisman, it has much to tell him, and we have little time."

Albert stopped shaking. He looked at Mr. Merwyn, studying his face. "Are you the Druid they spoke of?"

Mr. Merwyn nodded. "I am."

Albert's hand loosened its grip on my arm and fell away. "And you're ... old?"

Another nod. "I come from a time forgotten, when men cared for the Land and the Land cared for them. There was power in that bond of trust, power that grows weak as men put their trust in their own cleverness. They no longer care for the Land, only for their own creations. This will be their ruin. But the Talisman remains unchanged, it has the power to heal the Land. If you believe, if you allow it to return to its rightful place, the disaster you are courting may be averted."

Albert remained silent for a few moments, then he shook his head and rubbed his eyes. "You have fancy words, but they will not save my daughter."

"The Talisman will." Mr. Merwyn said. He raised his staff and pointed it at me, and when he spoke, I could tell he was speaking to me. "Let the boy look into it. His heart is true. It will show him what he needs to know."

Still, Albert hesitated.

"You haven't much time," Mr. Merwyn said. "Make your decision, and make it wisely."

# Chapter 39

## Mitch

The rain began to ease, but that was the only thing that was going right. The Princess kept sobbing and I couldn't get the sparks to light anything. No matter how hard I struck the flint, no matter how many sparks flew and landed on the small pile of threads and tiny bits of straw, they just glowed and faded away.

I struck harder and harder, getting more frustrated with each blow as the knowledge that it wasn't going to work solidified in my mind. I flung the rock against the wall and threw the cutter to the ground. Then I kicked the pile of kindling and sat with my head in my hands, not caring what the Princess thought.

She remained silent for a while. Her sobbing had stopped. When she spoke, she was right behind me. "You need a char cloth," she said.

For once, her voice wasn't mocking. I looked up at her. "A what?"

"A char cloth. I've seen the servants, when they need to use flint and steel, they spark onto a bit a burnt cloth."

I sighed. "Well, we don't—"

She held out her dress, where the embers had burned through. Around the holes, the fabric was scorched black. "I think this might work."

We set about collecting the kindling, making a small pile of straw, grass and thread. I found the flint and, using the sharp edge, cut the burnt fabric from her dress.

I held it up, examining it in the dim light. "So how does this work?"

She had me cut off a small, charred piece. Then she made a nest out of the kindling and placed the cloth inside it.

"Make some sparks," she said. "Try to get them to land on the cloth."

I hit the stone again. This time, when the sparks landed, they glowed, and remained glowing. She blew gently on the cloth, and the sparks glowed brighter. Then she picked up the nest and carefully folded it, so the glowing sparks were nestled inside. She blew on it again, and the inside of the nest glowed, and smoke began to rise from it, and then …

# Chapter 40

## Charlie

"Fire," I said. "I see fire."

This surprised me. Despite all the talk of true hearts, I had my doubts that it would work.

When Albert had nodded his grudging consent, he'd found a workman and ordered him to get the key to the display cabinet. He must have run both ways because he was back within a few minutes. Mr. Merwyn, in the meantime, disappeared, probably to his office, and returned as Mr. Merwyn. The difference was so remarkable that he needed to convince Albert, and John, of who he was. By then, the workman had brought the key and Mr. Merwyn opened the glass case.

"Pick up the stone," he said. "Look into it and tell us what you see."

And so, I stared at the stone. Or, more accurately, into it. I looked as deep as I could into the black hole, as my heart pounded and I felt sure it was going to come to nothing, but then, in the far distance, a light glowed, and grew brighter and then I saw fire.

"What else?" Albert asked, suddenly interested.

I strained my eyes. "There's a castle, with a train track running through it. And … and I see a hill, with a windmill on it. And there's a farm, with a storehouse. That's where they are being held! I see them! In the storehouse. And the storehouse is on fire."

I let go of the glass and jumped away. "We have to get to them, quickly!"

"But where?" Albert asked.

"I … I don't know," I said. "I only know what I saw. The castle, the windmill. They can't have gone to Holland already, can they?"

"You said the stone would show you what you needed to know," Albert said.

"Well, yeah. I've seen where they are, I just don't know where it is."

"This is a trick," Albert said. "You bring me here, raise my hopes with this nonsense, and tell me nothing. You will go back to the Tower!" He grabbed my arm and shook me, then swept his other arm toward John and Mr. Merwyn. "All of you, and without the salubrious surroundings you now find yourselves in. You will spend your lives in chains."

Albert grabbed for John, but instead of dodging away, John stepped forward, and looked directly at him. "I think I know where they are," he said.

Albert's grip tightened. "Another trick?"

"No," John said. "The castle and the tracks, that's the Clayton tunnel. I took a trip to Brighton one day and saw it. It was magnificent."

"But the farm?"

"There's a hill there, as well, very near the tracks, and there is a windmill on top of it."

"That's where they are," I said. "We have to go. Now."

Albert kept his grip tight. "But the farm. Where is the farm?"

"It shouldn't be hard to find," I said. "Just look

for a building that's on fire."

# Chapter 41

## Mitch

… a tiny flame popped into life from the centre of the nest.

"Oh," Vicky said, and dropped it.

I pushed the glowing bits together, added a tiny amount of straw and blew gently on it. The sparks glowed, then died.

I blew again.

They glowed, brighter this time. A tendril of smoke rose, but no flame.

I blew again. The sparks flickered, then died.

Vicky huffed and crossed her arms over her chest. She looked like she wanted to cry.

"That was brilliant," I said, before she could start.

"But it was a failure."

"Are you kidding? We had a flame. If we got one, we can get another. And we'll be ready for it next time."

"But we don't have much char cloth. There was only a bit."

I poked at the ashes. "We've still got some left."

"Still, what's the use …" Then she started sniffling.

"Don't start that, Vicky," I said, then slapped my hand over my mouth. "Sorry."

She sighed and rubbed away a tear. "No, that's all

right. You can call me Vicky, at least until I start acting like a princess."

I made no reply, but she began gathering up the tinder, carefully, methodically, weaving a new nest.

I looked up to the ceiling. The glow in the high windows told me day had begun. We were running out of time. Vicky placed the remaining char cloth in the nest, and I struck the cutter against the rock.

# Chapter 42

## Charlie

We left the Exhibition Hall in the carriage, taking the King's Road, because the public road was jammed. The carriage clattered over the cobbles as we got to Hyde Park Corner and entered the lane that took us through St. James's Park. It wasn't as crowded there, but people were already milling around under the trees or sitting by the side of the road or huddled under umbrellas in the half-light. Here, Albert told the driver to slow down, both for safety and so we didn't attract attention. I was burning with impatience, but I had to agree with him.

We trotted through drizzly dawn, down the tree-lined lane, until we entered an open space where a massive house sat. It was grey as the dawn, nearly blending into the cloudy sky, but it was magnificent, with columns and a big balcony. John said it was where the Queen lived, and stared, slack-jawed, at it. Mr. Merwyn just stared into the distance, unimpressed by the structure. We passed through a side gate, into a huge courtyard, where Albert, without a word, jumped out of the carriage and raced into the building.

"Where's he going?"

John shrugged. "He must be getting help."

"Or he's seeking to speak to someone," Mr.

Merwyn said, and went back to staring.

I looked around at the imposing building boxing us in on all four sides. "Well, I hope whoever he's going to see is easy to find, it would take half an hour to walk around this place."

We waited, nervous and anxious, for what seemed like ages. Then, Albert returned, dressed in old shoes, plain pants and a wrinkled, white shirt under a black vest. His moustache and sideburns now looked scruffy, and his wavy hair was hidden beneath a bowler hat.

"You stopped to change your clothes?" I said.

Albert rapped on the wall of the carriage, and we jerked forward. "It was necessary. I must remain incognito, and there were messages to deliver. We must keep the kidnappers unaware of our knowledge. My cousin will stand in for me at the ceremonies. He is almost my double; everyone will be looking at the Queen. No one will notice. Also, we have a stand-in for the Princess Victoria. The ceremonies will go ahead as normal."

"You changed your clothes," I repeated, "and you didn't stop to get any help."

We clattered along a lush park. In the distance I saw a lake with swans gliding over its ruffled surface. Not many people were around, however, given the early hour and our distance from the Crystal Palace.

"What happens today, no one must know about," Albert said at last. "Even if our mission is successful, it must not be known that the Royal family is so vulnerable."

"But surely, a guard or two—"

He held up a hand, the one with a large and gaudy ring on his index finger that he hadn't been wearing

211

earlier. "No one. My wife and I, and the kidnapers, are the only ones who know the whole truth. The driver knows only that he is taking me on an important, and secret, task. Any others we enlist will be likewise told. When this is over, however it ends, no one must know the whole truth."

I went a little cold and glanced at John, who was also looking doubtful. Mr. Merwyn kept staring, saying nothing. "All right," I said, but it didn't feel all right.

We left the park behind and galloped at an alarming pace through the wide streets. We careened through intersections, causing other carriages to pull their horses to a halt and people to jump out of the way. Then we came to the river, and a huge, ornate building that John called the Houses of Parliament. It looked like a cross between a Gothic cathedral and a shopping mall, with pointed spires, high windows and sections still under construction.

On the bridge, we swerved around other carriages and entered Southwark. The roads were wide and less crowded, so we made good time and were soon heading toward a building with a huge billboard outside of it reading, "Brighton, Croydon, Reigate and Epsom."

"It's London Bridge station," John said. "We can get a train to the Clayton Tunnel from here."

"Is there a station at the tunnel?" I asked.

"Well, no, but at least we can get there."

The carriage pulled up near the station office.

"Follow," Albert shouted, jumping from the carriage. "All of you."

We ran into the station office and were met by two startled clerks and a flabbergasted station master. And when Albert ordered him to get us a train, he became even more flabbergasted, especially when Albert showed him his ring and told him who he was.

"What you are asking is impossible," the red-faced man sitting behind the desk said. Then he suddenly stood up. "Your Majesty."

"Then make it possible," Albert said.

"But ... but, Your Majesty—"

The workday had barely begun. The trains were being fired up, but none had left the station. Spurred into action by the sight of Prince Albert, the station master began looking through ledgers and contacting other stations on the telegraph.

Using Royal Decree got us only so far, but Albert managed to move things along with promises of awards—monetary or honorary—for their help, and less desirable consequences for failure. It took nearly an hour of negotiation, cajoling and threats, but we got a train. Sort of. It was just an engine, pulling a coal car, manned only by the engineer, a fireman and a brakeman.

The plan was, to take the train to the Clayton tunnel, where it would stop and allow us to get off before continuing to Brighton. After we completed our unspecified—but highly sensitive and supremely important—mission, we would return to the tunnel. By that time, a north-bound train from Brighton would have arrived to pick us up and take us back to London. Once we arrived back at London Bridge Station, the service could begin normal operations. It wasn't a great plan, but it was the best we could cobble together.

All we needed was the authorization to put it in motion.

The station master, though frightened and eager to please, could not, on his own, make the decision. Wires and runners were sent to higher and higher authorities as the clock ticked. The rain stopped, the sun shone, and we waited. At nearly eight o'clock, the station master came to us, trembling and holding a sheet of paper with ink scribblings all over it.

"I have been contacted by members of the board of directors," he said. "Misters Samuel Laing and Leo Schuster have agreed to the, um, rescheduling of morning runs. But they have a condition."

Albert tapped his foot impatiently. "Out with it, then."

"They want, in return for this service, the Crystal Palace."

"What?" me and John said, unable to restrain ourselves.

Albert shook his head in disbelief. "But that is impossible. It's being opened this morning, and I can't simply give it away."

The station master ducked his head and turned white. "No, no your Highness. They mean after it closes. They want the building."

"But it belongs to the people. It would require an act of Parliament."

"Even so," the trembling station master said, "it is their condition."

"Very well," Albert said, turning away as if the matter had already been decided. "Tell them I will exert what influence I can to see that they are allowed to take over the building once the Exhibition is over."

We followed Albert out of the station to the platform.

"Get the train moving, now," he shouted. "Full

speed to the Clayton Tunnel."

We all climbed aboard. The whistle shrieked, the smoke billowed, the steam hissed, and the train lurched forward.

# Chapter 43

## Mitch

The first time must have been beginner's luck because I made spark after spark, and none caught. I was starting to despair and struggling to keep Vicky from seeing it when we finally got another hit.

This time, Vicky worked with more confidence, gently nursing the spark, enclosing it in the nest, blowing through the tinder, watching it smoulder.

Then the nest burst into flame.

She set it down and placed kindling on the flame.

When it grew large enough, I pushed the burning bits into the pile of cloth, wood shavings and straw we had laid up against the door. The fire caught and swirled upward, licking against the dry wood. Soon, I heard crackling and felt the heat. The door was beginning to burn.

The room grew bright, and warm, and filled with smoke, forcing us to move to the far wall.

"Those windows should vent the smoke," I said. "All we need to do is keep low and as far away from the fire as we can."

I made a few trips to throw more straw on the blaze and soon there was nothing left to feed the fire. But the door was burning, and the smoke, though thick up in the rafters, was venting out the windows, so the plan was working, at least that part of it.

"What happens when the door burns through?" Vicky asked. "How do we get through it if it's on fire?"

I stared into the flames. "I hadn't really thought about that," I said.

Soon, the door was fully engulfed. Then the doorframe caught fire, and the flames rose, crackling and sparking, and the sparks rose with the heat, swirling around the roof timbers.

Vicky saw it too. "What happens if the roof catches fire?" she asked.

I watched in horror as a tiny ember landed on a beam, and the dust, already heated by the fire below, began to burn. "I hadn't really thought about that, either," I said.

# Chapter 44

## Charlie

The going was slower than I would have liked, but once we left the built-up areas of the city, the engineer stepped on the gas. The rhythmic clacking of the rails got faster and faster until it was just one long rumble. The scenery whizzed by. The carriage shook. John went white.

There wasn't a lot of room, and we had to stay out of the way of the fireman and brakeman, so we squeezed up to the open edges of the engine cab, grabbed hold of whatever we could and held on. The cab, with the fireman shovelling coal into a gaping furnace, was like an oven, and stank of smoke and oil. Ashes whipped against my face as we sped through the countryside, shot through tunnels and screamed past stations where passengers waited, expecting us to stop. It was thrilling and terrifying at the same time, and I was amazed at how fast a steam train could go. I imagined the engineer was too. It was his chance to really open it up, and he grabbed it with enthusiasm.

We crossed a long bridge and saw some stunning views, but mostly we just hung on and hoped we would get there in one piece. And in time.

At last, the brakes squealed, and the train slowed, and the brakeman told us we could get out.

"This is where you wanted to be," he said. "Be

careful getting down, your Majesty."

Not being at a station, it was a jump to get to track level. We all made it, then stood on the edge of the embankment.

"Is this the place," Albert asked.

I looked around. The Clayton Tunnel, its opening built to resemble a castle, was in front of us. Off to the left, on top of a distant hill, I saw a windmill. "Yes, this is the place."

"Then where is your farm?"

# Chapter 45

## Mitch

Fire spread through the rafters with terrifying speed. The wood—centuries old and covered with dust and straw—fed the flames which scuttled along them, running further and higher and faster in a race to engulf every beam in the roof.

The air in the room became too hot to breathe and we choked on the smoke. Covering our faces with the blanket, we laid on the floor, trying to keep as far from the flames as possible.

I laid on top of Vicky in a futile attempt to protect her from the embers falling from above. The roar of flames engulfed me, and I knew we wouldn't last long. Beneath me, Vicky hacked and coughed.

"I'm sorry, Princess," I said.

"You can call me Vicky," she replied between gasps.

Then she fell silent.

I coughed, and things started to go black. Then I heard someone pounding on the door.

# Chapter 46

## Charlie

"There!" I pointed down the hill. The farm was nearby, a jumble of grey, stone buildings sprawled around a large farmyard. A two-story house sat at one end, with barns and various outbuildings at the other. One had smoke billowing from it. "Come on!"

We charged down the hill, through the brush and jumped over a stream where the land levelled and then rose to meet the farm. We scrambled up the incline, onto the hard-packed earth of the farmyard and rushed toward the burning building. Smoke poured from the high windows, flames sprouted from the roof and the only door was burning.

"They're in there!" I shouted.

In a panic, I grabbed an iron bar lying in the weeds and began pounding the door with it. Embers flew and the door rattled but stayed in place. I hit it again and again. It began to crumble in places, weakened by the fire. But the bar wasn't going to get the job done. Then I heard John calling from behind. "Over here, help us with this."

They had found a flat wheelbarrow, a long, broad platform mounted on a single set of wheels with handles at one end. Albert, Mr. Merwyn and John were pushing it forward, toward me and the door.

I jumped aside and ran around to help. We gained

speed and momentum and slammed into the door. It crumbled into a pile of embers and the cart stopped, half in and half out. Without hesitating, John jumped onto the cart and into the building. I followed.

It was like running into an oven. The heat and smoke hit me with a force that almost knocked me down. I struggled forward and bumped into John. "Where are they?"

I heard a faint cough somewhere in front of us.

"Over there," he said.

We scrambled forward on our hands and knees.

"Here," John said.

I reached toward him and felt a body on the floor. It was Mitch. He rolled toward me, opened his eyes and coughed. "What took you so long?" he rasped.

"I got the Princess," John said. He was already up, the Princess limp in his arms, running toward the door.

I grabbed Mitch by his arm. "Come on, get up, we need to get out of here."

He managed to stand with his arm over my shoulder and together we made for the door. We both hacked and coughed. Smoke stung my eyes and soon I could barely see. "Where's the door?"

"Somewhere in front of us," Mitch said.

We stumbled forward and tripped on the edge of the cart, falling face first onto it. Around us the embers were coming to life and flames licked the dry wood at the edges of the cart.

Then the cart shifted, levelled and jerked into the sunlight.

I blinked and looked up at John and Mr. Merwyn, each holding one of the cart's handles, pulling us into the farmyard, away from the burning building.

Nearby, Albert sat on the ground, holding the Princess, who was coughing and sputtering but seemingly all right, despite being dirty and dishevelled as a street urchin.

A roar erupted from behind and we all looked as the roof caved in and smoke, embers, and heat like a blast furnace belched out of the door opening.

Me and Mitch got off the cart and Mitch went to the Princess to see how she was while me and John stood with Mr. Merwyn.

The Princess hugged Albert. "Papa," she said, her voice raspy, "you came, I knew you would."

"It was these boys," Albert said, indicating us. "They saved you. Without them, I would not have been able to get to you. But you are safe now, mein juwel."

I let out a sigh. It was over, and I had an idea about how we might get the Talisman back. But Mitch didn't seem relieved. "The Opening Ceremony," he said to Albert, "did you call it off?"

Albert shook his head.

"You need to stop it!" Mitch said. "We need to get a message to London. Right now!"

Albert looked at him as if he was crazy.

"What are you talking about?" I asked.

Mitch looked in my direction and went white.

"Well, well," a voice said from behind. "Looks like you brought in reinforcements."

I turned. A man was coming toward us. He was unshaven, rumpled, and red-eyed. Around his neck was a silk scarf, on his head a bowler hat, and in his hands a rifle. And it was pointed at us.

# Chapter 47

## Mitch

It was the Jailer, and he wasn't wearing his mask. Vicky gasped, I froze, and the others looked on, concerned and apprehensive, but not as frightened as I was.

His gaze turned to me, Vicky, and then Albert. "And look what we have here, the Kraut Prince himself. I thought you were opening your dog and pony show this morning."

Albert looked up at him, wary, tensing for a fight. "My cousin is standing in for me, as I was too busy rescuing my daughter from traitorous scum."

The Jailer chuckled. "Bad luck for your cousin." He raised his rifle, pointing it at Albert. "But it gives me the pleasure of shooting you myself."

"No!" Vicky screamed, jumping in front of Albert as the rifle fired. The bullet slammed her body against Albert's and they both tumbled to the ground, Vicky's once-white dress turning crimson below her right shoulder.

I ran to her as Albert moved her off him and knelt by her side.

"Was that noble enough for you?" she asked, looking up at me. She coughed and blood ran down her chin.

"Oh, Princess, Princess, no."

"You can call me Vicky," she said.

"Mein Juwel!" Albert wailed.

I looked at the Jailer. He was raising the rifle again, pointing it at Albert's head. I turned to push him away. The rifle fired.

# Chapter 48

## Charlie

I saw the rifle buck in the man's hands as smoke and fire erupted from the barrel. The Princess, and Albert, fell to the ground, but in an instant, it became clear that Albert wasn't hurt. The Princess, however, was not so lucky.

In the seconds of shouting and wailing and screaming that followed, the man took aim again, and Mr. Merwyn swung his arm and threw something silver. Whatever it was hit the man smack on the forehead, and he fell back, the rifle firing harmlessly into the air.

John rushed in, grabbing the rifle. I ran to help, rolling the man over and pinning his hands behind his back. John found some rope and we tied the man up, while Albert, Mitch and Mr. Merwyn tended to the Princess.

"Hold this over the wound," I heard Mr. Merwyn say. "Press hard."

He was tearing off pieces of his shirt to make a bandage as Albert frantically pulled her ruffles and lace and ribbons away to get at her wound.

"You need to get her to the train, quickly," Mr. Merwyn said. He jumped up and ran. "I will meet you there. Go now."

We finished hog-tying the man and then retrieved

the ring of keys Mr. Merwyn had thrown. They'd done a good job of incapacitating the gunman, who was bleeding from a gash in his forehead. Me and John were going to sit him up and put him under a tree, but Mitch told us to leave him where he was. "Lying in the sun won't be as hot as a burning building," he said, "but it will be uncomfortable enough."

The Princess's breath became ragged, and she spit up blood every time she coughed. We put her on the cart and me, Albert and John pulled it toward the train while Mitch sat with the Princess, pressing the cloth to her wound.

The journey was a bumpy, difficult slog, and not as fast as any of us would have liked. On the way down the slope, Mitch, his voice still rasping, told us of the kidnaper's plans. Albert shook his head grimly, but merely said, "there is much to do when we return."

Mitch had to get off to help carry the cart over the stream and then help push it up hill. Albert carried the Princess for the final hundred yards and, at last, we arrived at the train as it chugged to a stop, just in time to meet us. This one had a passenger car attached, and we carried the Princess aboard and laid her on one of the bench seats.

As the train belched smoke and began to crawl forward, Mr. Merwyn raced up the hill and clambered aboard.

We all stood around the Princess, Albert stroking her hair, me and John just staring dumbfounded, and Mitch holding the bandage. Mr. Merwyn pulled a leather pouch from his pocket and, without a word, pushed Mitch's hand away and began applying a green paste to the wound.

227

"What do you think you're doing?" Albert demanded.

"This will slow the bleeding," he said, not looking up, "and it will calm her."

"I'll not have your superstitious potions used on my daughter!"

"It is not superstition. The Land will care for the child. But we must get her to London quickly."

"And I will take her to the Royal Surgeon as soon as we arrive There is no need for your primitive medicine."

"No," Mr. Merwyn said, looking up at Albert for the first time. "She must go to the Crystal Palace. The best surgeons in London are there, at the opening. You must get them. Bring them to the Queen's cloak room. Prepare it to receive her. These healing herbs will keep her alive until we get there, but then the surgeons must take over."

"You do not give me orders."

"If you value your child's life, you will listen to me, and do as I say."

Albert drew a breath, then looked down at the Princess's white face and let it out without saying a word.

"When we get to London," Mr. Merwyn said, "you will ride fast to the Crystal Palace. The Princess will follow in a carriage."

"I can't be hunting up doctors," Albert sputtered. "My wife is in danger. They are going to murder the Queen."

"Charlie and John will stop the assassin."

Albert looked at us doubtfully. "These, these … boys?"

"They are more capable than you give them credit

for. They saved your child. Trust them to save your wife, as well."

"What do I do?" Mitch asked.

Mr. Merwyn looked at him, then at the Princess. He paused, seemingly unsure of what to say. It was the first time I had seen him uncertain.

"You," he said to Mitch, "will get the Talisman."

# Chapter 49

## Mitch

The train travelled faster than I thought possible, covering the distance it had taken us two days to travel by cart in under an hour. Still, that was a long time, considering how bad Vicky was. Fortunately, Mr. Merwyn's potion seemed to sooth her. She was unconscious, but breathing normally and her wound wasn't spouting blood anymore.

As the train screamed over the track, we prepared ourselves for the tasks ahead, plotting the quickest route back to the Crystal Palace and how we were going to get to where we needed to go once we got there.

The Talisman, Mr. Merwyn told me, was the key. Its power could save her, and it was up to me to bring it to her.

I kept stroking Vicky's hair, talking to her softly, while Albert held the bandage. He wavered between looking at her with such deep sorrow it made me ache, and glancing around at us with barely disguised suspicion. I don't think he was fully on board with the Talisman idea, but he was so devoted to his daughter he had no option but to try whatever he could to save her, even believing us.

As the train pulled into the station, we all got ready. "Remember," Albert told Charlie and John, you must act discreetly. This plot must never become public knowledge. I must save my daughter, so you must save my wife. I am putting her life, and the Empire's future, in your hands. Do not fail."

He didn't say anything to me, though. I don't think he believed what I was doing was important.

Albert flung the door open before the train stopped, and jumped onto the platform, shouting for the station master to fetch a stretcher. We put Vicky on it. The station master took one end and Albert tried to take the other, but Mr. Merwyn pushed him aside. "Ride to the Crystal Palace. Quickly. Your daughter must have immediate attention as soon as she arrives. Make sure it is there for her."

Once again Albert's brow furrowed, but he looked at Vicky and turned away, toward me, Charlie and John. "Follow," he said. So, we did.

Outside the station, four horses—along with a carriage for Vicky and Mr. Merwyn—were hastily acquired, the task spurred by Albert's urgency as well as his position. The horse came to us saddled and ready, led by four young boys who whispered, "It's 'im, the Prince! It's really 'im!" as they approached. They helped us mount, Albert yanked the reins, gave his horse's flanks a kick, and was off.

We galloped after him, through the crowded streets, dodging carriages and pedestrians, taking side streets and alleys. Soon we crossed a bridge and were on the streets leading to the Crystal Palace, which were even more crowded. As we neared Hyde Park and the Exhibition, the crowds became so thick it was almost impossible to move. Albert jumped from his horse and collared a constable.

"You must clear a route, for a carriage, from the

Public Road to the northeast entrance. Make haste, the carriage will be arriving presently. It is of national importance."

The constable gaped at him. "Your Majesty!" Then he bowed. "I … that will be difficult. I'm just a constable. I don't have authority—"

"Do it," Albert said, jumping back on his horse.

The constable nodded and rushed away. We followed Albert, circling around the crowd until we found where it was thinnest. We pushed our way through with the horses as fast as we could, trying our best not to trample people. They didn't make it easy, though. Some of them couldn't, or wouldn't, get out of our way, and some even shouted at us to back off and wait our turn. Those were the people I didn't mind bumping with my horse as we rode by.

When the crush was finally too thick to push our horses through, we jumped off and barged our way toward the door. We were met by two guards, keeping the crowd at bay. They tried to push us back, but Albert identified himself and they ushered us inside, much to the dismay of the waiting crowd.

We ran past a tapestry exhibit and then entered the exhibitor's area where the general public wasn't allowed. At the far end was a room with a palace guard standing by the door. The guard stood aside for Albert, and we rushed inside. It was a sort of lounge, with sofas and big, ornate cabinets where coats and shawls and jackets hung from hangers. The walls were soft and white, covered in linen fabric, which gave a soothing feel to the room. There was also a table set for tea. Albert swept the table clean, sending the china cups and silver teapots crashing to the floor.

"This will be the operating table," he said, ripping

linen sheets from the wall. "Guard! Go to the Royal seats in the main hall. Find the Royal Surgeon. Bring him here. Be quick, and discrete!"

There was no time for pleasantries, so we left with the guard without a word to Albert. Then we raced into the main hall, past the elm tree and the crystal fountain, and a raised platform with an ornate chair on it. Just ahead, in a large, chaotic cluster, were the trappings for the opening ceremonies. The band, the choir, the platforms, and the guests of honour were all there, along with a huge crowd. but the Queen wasn't.

"The Queen," John said. "Are we too late?"

"The Queen," the breathless guard began, "and Prince Albert ... or ... who ...what is going on?"

"Never mind that," Charlie said, "where is the Queen?"

"The Royal family, and their entourage, are taking a grand tour of the exhibition. They have just left for the East Entrance and will walk the entire length of the Crystal Palace."

"That'll make finding him impossible!" Charlie said. "He could be anywhere."

"Who could be anywhere?" the guard asked. "You will tell me what is transpiring here. I demand an answer, in the name of the Queen!"

We all looked at him. "Why aren't you getting the Royal Surgeon," I said. "Like Prince Albert ordered you to."

The man blanched and ran off.

"He's probably in the gallery," John said. "He'll need to be up high to see her in the crowd."

Charlie shook his head. "We'll never find him in time. There's too big an area to search."

"If we split up."

"Still too big."

"No," I said. "There's to be a signal. That's what the kidnapper said. If the Queen agreed to the ransom, she was to sit in a chair. Otherwise, she was to walk past it. Either way, she would be in the assassin's line of fire. We need to find that chair, then we can find the assassin."

"They must have meant the one by the fountain," Charlie said. "So, he'll be somewhere around here."

"Some place high," John said.

We looked around. The gallery overlooked the main hall from every side. But there were throngs of people crushing against the railings. No place for a man to hide.

"Maybe the tree," John said uncertainly.

"Impossible," Charlie said.

But we all looked: up the trunk, through the lower branches, into the leafy middle and, finally, to the very top where, just visible between the leaves, was a man holding a rifle.

# Chapter 50

## Charlie

"This way!" John said.

"But the tree's that way," I said.

John didn't stop. "And how are you going to climb it?"

I ran after him. We kept to the side corridor, where the crowd was thinner, past farm machinery and into the maintenance area until we arrived at the storeroom.

"What are we doing here," I asked, as John raced around the room, flinging boxes open and tossing tools aside.

"Looking for …" He pulled out a coil of rope. "… this."

"What are you going to do?"

He jumped up and ran out the door. I raced after him.

"We can't climb the tree," he said, slamming through the nearest exit, "but we can drop down on it."

The guards at the door grabbed him. When I came up behind, they grabbed me too.

"Emergency maintenance," John said.

"We work here," I added.

The guards looked dubious, but, uncertain, they hesitated and loosen their grip. We took the opportunity to slip away and dash into the crowd.

"Hey, ho!" the guard yelled. "Stop those boys!"

But the crowd was only interested in what was happening inside. We slipped through the throng and John led me to the rear corner.

"This is how the maintenance men get up to fix the panels," he said, shouldering the rope.

There was a column at the corner, wider than the others, with narrow rungs like a ladder. John began climbing. "I hope you have a head for heights," he said.

I gulped down my rising dread and climbed up after him.

# Chapter 51

## Mitch

John and Charlie ran one way, I ran the other, toward the display where the Talisman was. It was hard going until I bulled my way through the crowd, crossed the corridor and ducked into the back passages of the south side. They were practically empty, with the spectators all cramming toward the main corridor to see the Queen pass by.

I ran on, unhindered, wondering how I was going to get it out of its case. I was thinking about where I could find something to smash the glass with, but as the Talisman exhibit came into view, that problem disappeared, only to be replaced by another: standing in the corridor, in front of the Talisman, was Farran. And he had a brick in his hand.

I ran faster. He turned, alerted by the sound of my feet pounding on the boards. "It's mine!" he shouted, and threw the brick.

The glass case shattered. He leapt forward and, with a cry of glee, snatched the Talisman from its velvet pillow. I pushed harder. Farran turned and ran. I dove, landed hard on the floor, and grabbed him by an ankle.

He slipped from my grip, but his feet tangled, and he hit the floor, his arms and legs splayed out like a starfish. The Talisman bounced out of his hand and rolled away. We both saw it and scrambled after it. I grabbed his leg, but he kicked me away. I sprang forward and he caught hold of my suspenders, pulling me back. We rolled, wrestled, kicked, bit, and scratched, and all the while kept striving toward the Talisman as it rolled lazily along the floor. Then we both froze and watched in horror as the Talisman wavered, slowed, turned slightly to the left and slipped into the gap between the floorboards.

# Chapter 52

## Charlie

When we reached the top of the first level, I felt dizzy from the height, but John didn't hesitate, he took off, running across the beam to where the second tier rose. By the time I caught up with him, he was already halfway up the wall. I looked down, immediately regretted it, and climbed after him. At the top of the second tier was yet another one. We scaled that and sat on the beam, winded and a little giddy from the ascent. A hundred yards away, glowing in the noon sun, rose the barrel-vaulted roof of the transept.

If this had been a normal roof, getting to the transept would have been easy, but the beam we had to walk across was bounded on either side by glass, meaning I had to cope with seeing ant-sized people, and know that, if I fell, I—along with razor-sharp shards of glass—would plummet a hundred feet into the teaming ant-colony below. So, I walked, my heart in my throat and my eyes staring straight ahead, putting one foot in front of the other, taking one step at a time toward the transept, where John was waiting for me. When I got there, John allowed me a moment to catch my breath, then he climbed the ladder leading to the top of the arch. And I followed.

We crawled along the top beam. Below us we saw

the ceremonial platforms and the waiting crowds, then the crystal fountain, and then the tree where the man crouched, hidden, holding a rifle by his side. Behind us, the central hall began to clear. Guards pushed the crowds away as people in the corridors and gallery strained forward. A roar, that had been dull and distant, became deafening. I looked to the corridor and caught a glimpse of the Royal procession.

"The Queen's coming," I said.

Directly below us, through the leafy canopy, we saw movement. The man with the rifle was taking aim.

# Chapter 53

## Mitch

"NOOOOOOO!" Farran screamed, as it disappeared.

He pushed me away and scrambled to the spot where the Talisman had slipped through the gap. Whimpering and moaning, he tried to shove his fingers through the slit.

I jumped up and ran. Farran paid no attention. I raced down the corridor and slammed through the exit, startling the guards, and ran around the corner of the building. Then I moved along the side until I thought I was in line with the Talisman exhibit and climbed under the structure.

Scrambling through the low space, crawling over nails, screws and bits of broken glass mixed with dust and debris, I made my way toward where I thought the Talisman had fallen. It was such a big, dark space that finding it was going to be impossible. Then I heard Farran, scratching and shouting. I moved toward the sound until he was nearly above me. There, lying on the ground, was the Talisman. I scooped it up and made for the far side.

"Give it back," Farran screamed. "It's mine"

He crawled along with me, keeping me in sight. I veered to the right, under exhibits that he had to go around, but he found me again, tracking my path. In the main corridor, he crawled through the crowd, pushing people out of his way. I moved to the left and scrambled forward.

I don't know if I lost him or not, but it didn't matter, there was no way for him to get at me. I crawled out from under the structure, stuffed the Talisman in my pocket and ran for the entrance.

It was still crowded, but not like it had been, and when I rushed through the entrance I discovered why. The crowd was pressing into the middle to get a glimpse of the Queen, giving me a clear path to the room Vicky was in. I ran toward it. Then something hit me. Hard.

I dropped to my knees, gasping, my shoulder and side screaming in pain. I tried to stand, but blackness enveloped me, and I slumped to the floor.

# Chapter 54

## Charlie

"We've got to stop him," John said. "Break the glass."

I grabbed his raised fist. "No. There are people down there. And it won't stop him, it will just alert him. He'll still shoot the Queen, and then us."

"Then what do we do?"

I felt in my pocket. "This," I said, holding up the glass cutter.

I scored a panel near one of its corners, making a triangle. Holding my breath, I tapped the glass. It split along the line and hung down, held to the iron frame by the putty. I pulled it out and, putting our hands through the hole, we loosened and lifted the entire pane of glass.

"Tie the rope to the girder," I said, laying the glass aside.

John tested the knot. I threw the rope through the opening, grabbed hold of it and began to climb down, with John right behind me.

I went as fast as I could, hand under hand, but it wasn't fast enough. The Queen approached the fountain, looked at the chair, and walked past it. I slid, using the rope like a fireman's pole. My hands burned, my legs ached. The assassin took aim. I let go of the rope and dropped like a stone into the tree.

I landed on his back and grabbed him around the neck, not so much to stop him, but to save my own life. His rifle pointed skyward and fired. The sound boomed in my ears. A hole appeared in one of the roof panels, but the crowd below, lost in their thunderous euphoria, noticed nothing.

Then I fell—along with the rifleman and the rifle—through the branches.

We bounced from one limb to the other. I grabbed one to break my fall, slipped and bumped into another. The assassin hit a branch and folded over it like a wet dish rag, the rifle slipping from his hand. I grabbed another branch and hung, scrambling to find a place to put my feet, my other hand swinging wildly through the air and grabbing nothing. I began to slip.

Then hands grabbed my arm and held me. I clutched the branch and looked up at John.

"Come on," he said. "Let's get out of this tree."

We climbed down the branches, then slid down the trunk. In the corridor, the crowds cheered, the procession carried on. No one had noticed a thing.

Then I saw Mitch, lying on the floor with a rifle by his side.

# Chapter 55

## Mitch

The next thing I knew, someone was helping me up, and my side felt like it was on fire. I winced and shook my head, trying to drive away the dizziness.

"Are you alright?"

Charlie's voice.

"Someone hit me."

"No," another voice said.

I looked and saw it was John, holding a rifle. "It was this. The assassin dropped it. You're lucky it didn't hit you on the head."

I took a tentative breath and felt my aching ribs. "I don't feel so lucky."

"Can you walk?" Charlie asked.

I nodded. "I think so."

"Then come on. We've got to get to Albert."

But before I could take a step, another blow knocked me to the floor. I fought off the blackness and saw Charlie and John, both on the floor next to me. My hands were twisted behind my back and manacled.

Someone above me spoke. "Assassins!"

We were pulled to our feet. Three burly policemen held us. Then I heard another voice. "I always knew you three were up to no good."

It was Morgan.

# Chapter 56

## Charlie

"We're not assassins," I said. "Look up in the tree, that's where the assassin is." But they were already pulling us away.

"Shut your gob," Morgan said. "Your days of spinning tales are over. It's the gallows for you."

I tried the constable who was dragging me. "Just look up. He's in the tree." But all that got me was a rough shake and a smack across the face.

The crowd in the transept surged down the corridor, following the Queen. It was still mobbed with people, but the policemen bulled their way through. No one took notice of us and, in fact, seemed determined not to acknowledge that four burly men were carting three boys away in handcuffs.

They half-dragged us across the corridor, toward the entrance, fighting the flood of people streaming in.

"Take them to the station," Morgan said. "Lock them up and guard them. They are slimy characters."

We were passing the room Albert had prepared for the Princess. In a moment we would be outside, swallowed up in the crowd, and we would simply disappear. There was nothing we could do, but I had to do something.

"Not as slimy as your friends," I said to Morgan.

"You met with the assassins in the workshop and made a deal with them. I was there. I heard you."

Morgan paused and looked at me. "What did you say?"

The constable gripping my arm gave me another shake, making my teeth rattle and the manacles dig into my wrists. "Shut yer gob!"

They started pulling us again. I took a breath. "It doesn't matter, Mr. Morgan. You'll be reunited with them soon enough."

"What is he prattling on about?" one of the other constables asked. This one had a stripe on his sleeve. The other officers stopped and looked at him, then at Morgan.

"He's just spinning tales," Morgan growled. "Give 'im 'ere. I'll sort 'im out."

The constable shoved me toward Morgan, who grabbed me by the throat and dragged me a short distance away, just far enough to be out of earshot of the group, but in a position where I could still see the door to the room where the Princess, Albert and Mr. Merwyn were. "What are you playin' at?"

I made a few strangled sounds. Morgan let go of my throat. "The people you met with in the workshop. You did them a favour, allowing them to steal a jewel."

Morgan's face went red. "Why you lyin'—"

"Only they didn't steal a jewel. Their plan was to assassinate the Queen. We stopped them. They'll be arrested, and encouraged to tell who helped them."

The red slowly drained from Morgan's face, leaving it a pasty white. "Then maybe I'll have to arrange for a little accident to befall you and your friends."

"Kill us if you want," I said, glancing toward the door. "But you'll still be caught."

Morgan smiled. "If that's the case, then I may as well get what satisfaction I can."

He looked up at the constable with the stripe. "I've had enough of their lies. Gag them, all of them!"

Handkerchiefs appeared, and the constables tied them over Mitch and John's mouths. Morgan pulled a dirty, crumpled one from his pocket and pulled it into a taught rope. As he leaned near, I saw a movement out of the corner of my eye. It was Albert, entering the office with three men in formal suits and top hats. I opened my mouth to scream. Morgan shoved the gag in and cinched it tight.

"Come on," he said dragging me back to the group. "I think maybe we need to take a detour on the way to the station."

We were almost through the entrance when a voice called out. "What is going on here?"

"None of your concern, sir," the head constable said. "Go back to your celebration."

"This is my hall, and he is my head of security, so it is certainly of concern to me."

Then Mr. Paxton stepped in front of the group, forcing us to a halt. Morgan, blanched.

"We found these miscreants, Mr. Paxton," Morgan stammered. "We believe they are wanted. For murder. And they had this rifle. They are clearly up to no good."

Mr. Paxton looked us over. "They don't appear to be of that ilk. What did they say when you arrested them?"

"They gave us a fairy story, sir," the striped constable said. "Told us a man in the tree dropped it on them."

"Was there a man in the tree?" Paxton asked. "Did you look?"

The constable's face went red. "Well, no, sir."

"Then do so. Now."

He and one of the constables ran off. Mr. Paxton looked at Morgan. "Ungag them."

"With respect, sir," Morgan said. "I'd rather not. The gags are to keep them from telling lies."

"These boys," Mr. Paxton said, "are my employees, and until I have reason to believe otherwise, I will consider them loyal and truthful. Now take off the gags."

The gags came off. We all sputtered and drew a few deep breaths.

"Mr. Paxton," I said. "You need ... I need to ask you one last favour. If you believe us like you say, that room over there ..." I turned and pointed with my manacled hands. "... if you go there, you'll meet a man who will explain all of this."

Mr. Paxton rubbed his chin. "And whom, may I ask, will I be meeting?"

"I can't tell you, sir. If I did, you would think I was lying, but I assure you, if you go and see him, everything will be made clear."

"Now you do stretch your credibility," Mr. Paxton said.

"It's only a little favour," John said.

"And he is telling the truth," Mitch added.

Morgan grabbed the back of my neck and shook me like a rag doll. "That was why we gagged them, Mr. Paxton."

Then the constable returned, pushing his way through the crowd, his face white and sweating.

"There was a man," he said. "Sergeant Bickson is getting him down now. He needs our assistance."

"Well," Mr. Paxton said. "I see no reason to not believe them."

He turned to go. "But Mr. Paxton, surely you're not—"

"I surely am," Mr. Paxton said without turning. "And constables, please remain with the boys until I return. See that no harm comes to them."

It got really awkward after that. The constables were itching to go, Morgan was itching to throttle us, and we were sweating out the wait, knowing that, if it went wrong, we were heading for prison, or worse.

When Mr. Paxton finally returned, he looked in shock. "Release these boys immediately," he barked.

The constables removed the manacles. We rubbed our sore wrists while Morgan protested, and Mr. Paxton ignored him.

"Constables, go and help your sergeant," Mr. Paxton said. "Mr. Morgan, you go with them and report to me later. I have official duties yet to perform."

And with that, he was off, once again looking calm and in control. The constables, one still carrying the rifle, left and, after a few moments of glaring at us, Morgan followed.

# Chapter 57

## Mitch

We pushed through the crowd and entered the room. Mr. Merwyn and Albert stood just inside the door watching three men bending over the table with the drape on it. On the table, covered with a sheet, was Vicky. Her ruined dress lay on the floor, burnt, bloody and torn.

The men—doctors, I assumed—poked and prodded and whispered among themselves. Then one came our way, a look on his face that alternated between sorrow and panic.

"How is she?" Albert asked, displaying a calm he struggled to maintain.

"It's a miracle she made it this far," the doctor said. "The poultice you put on her, Mr. Merwyn, it saved her life."

"So, she is to recover?" Albert asked.

The doctor sighed. "We got the bullet out, but she has lost a lot of blood. And there is bleeding inside that we cannot stop. I am afraid there is little hope."

Albert turned grey, but he drew a sharp breath and stood erect. "Can I see her."

The doctor looked away. "I think you should."

"Her mother—"

"Would not get here in time, I fear."

I felt Mr. Merwyn's hand on my shoulder. "Take

the Talisman to her."

I took a step forward. Albert shot me a look. "What do you think you are doing? Out, all of you, I want to be with my daughter."

"The Talisman will save your daughter," Mr. Merwyn said.

"I've had enough of this superstitious nonsense. Leave me to grieve in peace."

His head drooped, and he covered his eyes with his hand. I took the opportunity to dash for the table. The doctors tried to block me. I dodged around them, and they grabbed me by the collar. Straining forward, I pulled the Talisman from my pocket and grabbed Vicky's hand. It was limp and cold. Albert came marching toward me, his face red. The doctors had my arm now, trying to break my hold on Vicky without pulling her off the table. With my free hand, I slipped the Talisman into her palm and closed her fist around it.

Albert's hand slammed down on my back, gripped my shirt and yanked me backward. The doctors shrank away as he screamed, "Away from her! Get away from her!"

I allowed myself to be pulled away, hoping it would calm him, but there were more shouts and accusations, and the doctors joined in, scolding me for intruding, and Charlie and John grabbed Albert, trying to make him let go of me.

"Papa?"

We all froze.

"Papa, is that you? Are you safe?"

Albert let go and ran to the table. "Yes, mein juwel, I am here, I am safe, as are you."

"I'm shot, Papa," she said. Her voice was barely a

whisper, but her white cheeks began to colour and she drew a deep breath. "Am I dying?"

Albert held her hand, the one that held the Talisman. "I think not, mein juewl."

The doctors returned to the table. Ignoring Albert, they looked at her wound and checked her breathing and her pulse. "It is a miracle," one of them said. The others looked at him with disapproval.

The doctors tucked the sheet around her. "We need to leave her now. She needs rest."

Albert kissed Vicky's forehead as the doctors moved him away. They ushered us out the door, and came with us, closing the door behind them. We stood, silent as sentries, waiting.

After a few minutes, Albert turned to the doctors. "And what is your prognosis now?"

Two of the doctors coughed nervously and looked away. The one who had called it a miracle looked at Albert. "I am a man of science," he said, "I deal in knowledge, facts, proven processes, but as a doctor, I see miracles every day. Your daughter is young and strong and, importantly, believes in the charm that boy gave her. I think that was enough to pull her through. The bleeding has stopped, her pulse and breathing are normal. She simply needs rest."

"I must tell her mother," Albert said. "You will care for her."

"Yes, Your Majesty," the doctors said.

He turned to us. "And you will stay?" It was less of an order and more like a plea.

"Of course," I said.

The doctors went back into the room and Albert, oddly, walked out the front entrance.

"He'll be going back to Buckingham Palace," John

253

said, when he saw my questioning look. "He can't go see the Queen while she's here, because he's already with her."

"Yeah," Charlie said, "two Albert's would be too much for the crowd."

"And for me," I said.

I felt relieved, and more relaxed than I had in days. The Queen was safe, Vicky was going to live, and we had the Talisman. But Mr. Merwyn remain tense.

"Is something wrong?" I asked him.

He kept staring, as if he was looking for something in the far distance. "Something is wrong, something is terribly wrong. I see dark things ahead, unimaginable things …"

His words frightened me. "But the Talisman," I said, hoping to cheer him up. "We have it now. We can return it to the Sacred Tor."

This only made his brow furrows deepen. "That is not yet true. It still belongs to the Monarchy. And I fear I have made an unwise decision. I was swayed by the bravery of the girl's sacrifice. I chose the easy path. I should have let her die."

"What!?"

"I feel an emptiness, and darkness ahead, engulfing the Land—"

"But, the Talisman," I insisted. "We still have a chance to get it, don't we?" But even as I spoke the words, I began to feel the emptiness and glimpse the darkness, and my heart turned to ice.

"The Talisman," I said, but not to Mr. Merwyn. I grabbed Charlie and John and pushed them toward the door.

"What's going on?" John asked.

We barged through the door. The small crowd

254

surrounding Vicky's bed looked up. There were more doctors, and other men, attending her, as well as a few women, probably her servants. She was sitting up, leaning against a mountain of pillows—her cheeks rosy, her hair combed—wearing a frilly dressing gown. A princess again. Then I saw another door, one I hadn't noticed before.

"Princess," I said, relieved in spite of my growing misgivings, "you look well."

She inclined her head toward me. "Thanks to you." She looked to John and Charlie. "And to you, as well. My family, the Nation, the Empire, have much to thank you for."

"The Talisman," I said. "Could we have it back?"

She looked at me quizzically. "But I already gave it to you."

"No," I said. "You didn't."

She reddened slightly. "Well, not to you, but a doctor came to me, and said you wanted it back. I gave it to him. I assumed he gave it to you."

"One of these doctors?"

"No. One I hadn't seen before. He was tall and thin, with dark hair."

Charlie looked at me. "Fallan,"

I felt the colour drain from my face.

"Is it gone, then?" Charlie asked, his face also white.

One of the doctors cleared his throat. "I shouldn't worry about it if I were you," he said, his voice, as well as his eyes, looking down at us. "Granted, belief in the stone had a mild placebo effect, and that helped her Royal Highness to rally, and gave us time to bring in the surgeons who saved her."

"The Talisman is what saved her," Charlie said. "It

saved her twice, once when it showed me where she was, and again after she was shot."

The doctor chuckled. "Believe what you will, but I prefer to put my trust in our modern advances."

"And that will spell your doom."

I looked up. Mr. Merwyn had joined us, his face grey. The doctor looked at him. "I would ask you to leave this room at once. This is—"

"You forsake the Land at your peril. Progress without purpose, progress without concern for the Land that nurtures and protects you, progress for the sake of progress, therein lies darkness and destruction."

"Someone have that man ejected," the doctor said, his voice rising. "Better yet, have him arrested."

Mr. Merwyn ignore him. "Desolation awaits you. Unless the Talisman is returned to the Sacred Tor, the Land, and all you know, will be swept away."

"Guards, police, somebody!"

"I must go now," Mr. Merwyn said. "I must amend for my error. I must find the Talisman."

"We'll come with you," Charlie said.

Mr. Merwyn shook his head. "No, this is a quest I, alone, must undertake. You must return, safe, to your homes."

"What about the cloak?" I asked. "Will we need it again?"

But Mr. Merwyn was already walking away, out the open door.

"Wait," Charlie said. "Don't go."

We ran through the door.

"I can't see him," John said. "Where'd he go?"

I scanned the thinning crowd. He was nowhere to be seen.

# Chapter 58

## Charlie

They took the Princess away shortly after that, carried on a stretcher lined with pillows, and covered in a blanket, with only her face showing. She and Mitch had a quick good-bye. I think it might have been a sappy hug-fest, but the Talisman episode soured the mood. Still, they exchanged promises to never forget each other, and she thanked us all for our service to her and the Empire.

After our good-byes, the Royal Guards carried her through the entrance where a carriage waited, leaving us alone in the surging crowd.

"Is that it?" John asked. "Did we just go through all of that, and now we just go back to work?"

I looked at the finely dressed crowd, marvelling at the Exhibition that we, in a very small way, had helped to open. It had been a success. The Queen was safe. The Princess was back where she belonged. And Mr. Merwyn was gone. The last thought caused a tug in my chest. Our work here was finished. I knew we would be going home soon.

"I don't know," I said. "We worked for Mr. Merwyn, and he's gone. There's nothing more for us to do here."

Mitch nodded, but John looked doubtful. "You're going home, then?"

"Yes," Mitch said.

"But we need to wait for Albert. He asked us to, and we promised we would."

I sighed. "I'll give him an hour.

We didn't need to wait that long. About fifteen minutes later, two Palace Guards led us to the King's Road where a carriage waited. It was ornate, and comfortable inside, with cushioned seats and curtained windows. We travelled the short distance from the Crystal Palace to the real palace—the one John called Buckingham—where men, dressed in what I expect even John considered to be old-fashioned outfits, escorted us across the courtyard and into a gaping entrance hall.

I expected to be bowled over, but in comparison to the Crystal Palace, Buckingham was dark, and the rooms and hallways—immense as they were—still made you feel boxed in, unlike the transparent walls and ceiling we'd been used to. And the place smelled of smoke.

The guards led us to a set of double doors and positioned us, standing shoulder to shoulder, in front of them. "Do not speak unless asked a direct question," one of them said, while the other snatched John's cap off his head and handed it to him. He didn't bother with me or Mitch because we'd both lost ours. Then, with practice flair, they flung the doors open.

The room was brighter than the hallway, lit by huge windows which illuminated the large sofa at the far end where Albert and a woman sat. Albert was now in his royal clothes—thigh-high boots, blue trousers, frilled white shirt covered by a red jacket. The woman was short and, to be polite, sturdy. She was dressed in an ornate gown with a fur shawl draped over her shoulders. Her lips seemed to turn down in a perpetual frown, but you could see that, at one time, she had been beautiful. She had pearls and a tiara in her hair.

We walked toward them, escorted by the guards, our feet clacking on the black and white marble tiles. When we got to within ten feet of them, the guards made us stop. John bowed, so we did too.

"Her Majesty the Queen," one of the guards said, his voice booming through the hall. "And His Royal Highness Prince Albert of Saxe-Coburg and Gotha."

After a few awkward moments, the Queen waved us forward. "You may approach," she said, looking at us as if we were interesting, but decidedly odd, scientific specimens. "I understand you had something to do with assisting the Princess Royal."

If "something" meant almost getting burned to death and kidnapped and held prisoner and knocking an assassin out of a tree and getting the Talisman to the Princess in time to save her life, then, yeah, we had something to do with it.

"Yes, Your Majesty," we said.

"Then you are commendable young men, and you have our thanks," she said, somehow making the compliment sound like a dismissal. The guards prodded us and, following John's example, we, and the guards, walked backward, away from the Royal couple.

Albert held up a gloved hand. "Should we not show our appreciation in some way?"

We halted. The Queen scowled at Albert, but he ignored her and continued. "A monetary show of appreciation, perhaps."

"Whatever for?" the Queen snapped. "They have our thanks."

"To compensate them for their …efforts, and any inconveniences suffered." He gazed directly at us as he said this, giving us a look that suggested the Queen hadn't been fully briefed.

"And what would one give as compensation for efforts and inconveniences?" the Queen asked Albert.

"I should think one hundred pounds."

The queen's frown deepened. That seems a considerable—"

"Each."

John gasped. We shrugged. The Queen harrumphed and waved her hand in our direction to dismiss us, once again.

"Very well," she said. "Give them each one hundred pounds."

"Thank you, your Majesty," John said, unable to contain himself.

The guards nudged him, and the Queen scowled again, so I said, "Yeah, thanks!" then Mitch stepped forward.

"If I may," he said.

The Queen looked shocked, and one of the guards went to grab Mitch by the back of the neck, but Albert raised his hand again.

"You may," he said. "Now speak."

"The Talisman," Mitch said. "It is missing. And we need to find it."

"That has little to do with us," the Queen said.

"Of course, your Majesty," he said, making a slight bow. "It is our task to find it. But, um, tradition holds that it belongs to the Crown. If we do find it, and have it in our possession, it would be best if it rightfully belongs to us."

The Queen sat up a little straighter. "And who might you be?"

"We are the Guardians of the Talisman," he said. I wanted to drop through the floor, but the Queen seemed intrigued. "We presented it to Queen Elizabeth because, at that time, it was the right thing to do. But we need it returned, if we are to take it to the Sacred Tor, so it can guard the Land."

The Queen stared at Mitch for what seemed like an hour, though it was probably only about fifteen seconds. She started to say something, stopped, pondered some more, then said, "It is missing, you say?"

"Yes, your Majesty."

She flicked her hand again, dismissing us once more.

"Then it is no good to us. You may have it."

"Thank you, your Majesty" Mitch said, as the guard pulled him backward.

They couldn't get us out of the room fast enough.

In the hallway, we were met by a servant holding a silver tray with three fat envelopes on it. The envelopes were of fine, stiff paper and had our names written on them. Inside each was a hundred pounds in large, bulky notes, and a letter, signed by Albert, instructing anyone we showed it to, to provide us safe passage and any help we desired.

"He had this all set up before he even mentioned it to the Queen," Mitch said, reading the letter for the second time.

"He must know how to handle her," I said, stuffing the money into my pocket. "I know I wouldn't want to try."

John just stared, open-mouthed, at the envelope, the letter and the money.

The guards escorted us into the courtyard, bypassing the carriage that was still there, and led us to an outer door, holding it open and obviously expecting us to leave on foot. I held the letter up to one of them. "Doesn't this mean you should give us a lift to the station?"

# Chapter 59

## Mitch

We took the four o'clock train back to Horsham, riding in a first-class carriage.

The only trouble we had was trying to buy tickets with such large bills, because there wasn't enough money in the till to make change. So, the ticket clerk called the station master, who recognized us, and when I showed him my letter from Albert, he put us in first-class. Free of charge.

This wasn't the best choice. In a train carriage with suited gentlemen and dressed up ladies sitting on cushioned seats, three dirty, scruffy and smelly boys drew a good deal of unwanted attention. But when they found out we had been at the opening of the Crystal Palace, and had even worked there, they wanted us to tell them all about it.

At Three Bridges, they waved to us as we left the train, and the station master shook our hands. A very different greeting than we'd received when we first arrived, and a decidedly more pleasant return journey.

From there, we took the train to Horsham, and walked to Esther's house, but when John tried to go in, he found the door locked. Puzzled, he knocked. No one came. Then a woman passing by stopped.

"You won't find anyone there, sonny. Old Farran evicted the widow and her child."

"Where can we find her?" John asked.

The woman glared at him from beneath the rim of her grey cap. "Why, you looking for money, as well?" She stepped closer. "Oh, you're the boy. Her nephew. I dare say, she's been worried sick about you."

"Do you know where she is?"

"Staying with Mrs. Tompkins, last I heard."

"Thank you," John said, jumping off the steps. He rushed past the woman, up the street.

"Yeah, thanks," we said, following him.

We found Aunt Esther, along with Maggie, Mrs. Tompkins, and her husband, in a small house down the lane. It was cramped, crowded with washing buckets and drying laundry, and smelled of mildew.

Esther looked tired, but her eyes lit up when she saw John. She threw herself at him and enveloped him in a hug. "You're safe!" She said. "Mr. Farran was desperate to find you. I was so afraid."

"You lost your home," John said.

Esther waved her hand as if it was of no consequence. "He'd have found a reason to turn us out sooner or later. The important thing is, you're safe."

She hugged us too. Then Maggie overcame her shyness and we all hugged again. And, of course, when we were properly introduced to Mrs. Tompkins and her husband, the hug-fest started again.

Mr. and Mrs. Tompkins didn't have much, but they were generous. We took baths, while they heated up buckets of hot water for us, and Esther gave us back our clothes, cleaned and ironed. It felt odd wearing modern clothes after all that time. Odd, but nice.

Mrs. Tompkins thought we looked strange, but

264

Esther explained that this was how people dressed where we came from, and she didn't mention it again.

After that, we had a meal—a simple stew that tasted divine—with all seven of us crowded around a small table. While we ate, we told them about our adventures in London and at the Crystal Palace. Well, most of them, anyway. After that, it was time to leave. Esther brought out our cloak and, having contrived to say a private good-bye to us, was able to give it to us without causing Mr and Mrs. Tompkins to raise their eyebrows.

"Go home," she said, hugging us again. "But come back. Next time we will be ready for you."

"We borrowed money from you," I said. "Before we go, we need to pay it back."

I handed her the hundred pounds. Her face turned scarlet. "Oh, no, I can't take this. Really, I can't—"

"We owe it to you," Charlie said. "This much, and more." He placed his hundred pounds on top of mine.

"But, I can't—"

"Yes, you can," I said.

"And here's what I owe you," John said. "For room and board." He laid another note on top of the growing pile. "You won't have to live here anymore. You can get your own place, start your business up again."

Esther looked at the money. "With this, I could buy my own house." Then a smile spread across her face. "And I know just the one."

When we finally did leave, the sun was setting. We walked through the town as the evening drew in, and the few people who were in the street were too tired from the day and too eager to get home to worry

265

about what we looked like.

We came to the crossroad, and the Green Dragon pub, turning onto the road that led to the collection of houses that John told us was called Broadbridge Heath. Horsham had expanded since we'd previously seen it in 1588, and now there were more houses, and a second pub—The King's Arms—on the road out of town. Soon, however, the landscape returned to greenery, and I began to enjoy the solitude. It felt good to simply walk and not have to be afraid, surrounded by fields, cows, and a silence broken only by an occasional moo and the singing of crickets.

John, though becoming used to the mystery that surrounded us, remained sceptical about our plan to return home.

"You're just gong to crawl under that cloak and—poof—you'll go back to the future?"

"Well, it's not really that simple," I said. "We'll need to fall asleep, first."

"Why?"

"We don't know, that's just how it works."

"So, you don't understand this any more than I do?"

I shook my head. "Not really."

"But you do live in the future?"

I nodded.

"What can you tell me about it?"

"Well …"

Would it do any good? He'd never believe the technology, and there were a lot of bad things that he didn't need to know about. At last, I said, "You become our great-great-great-great-grandfather."

He pondered for a moment, then smiled. "Really?"

"Yes, really."

By the time we reached the crossroad at the village of Broadbridge Heath, it was nearly dark. As we turned down the road that would lead us home, the few people who were out on the street waved and wished us good evening. It was peaceful and calming. So calming that, when a horse came clopping up behind us, we didn't bother to look. Then it stopped.

"Returning to the scene of the crime, eh?" We turned and saw Farran, dismounting from a black horse, a cosh already in his hand.

I got ready to run, but John stood his ground.

"We've nothing to fear from you now," he said. "We're not in debt to you, and we've done no wrong. You are the thief."

Farran smiled. "Don't fear me, eh? Well, fear this."

He lunged forward, swinging the cosh. We scattered. John dodged just beyond Farran's reach as we ran behind him. He turned, swinging toward us, and John tripped him. As Farran sprawled out on the road, John jumped up and landed on his chest with both knees.

"Hey," Charlie said. "You told me not to do that!"

John jumped off Farran, who flopped around on the road, gasping. "I don't care if I kill him," he said.

"He took the Talisman," I said. "Search him."

We turned out his pockets, checked his coat, his purse, scattering his belongings and money over the muddy road.

"It's not here!"

We checked to see if there was a bag on the horse. There wasn't. Then Farran struggled to his knees.

"Help," he screamed. "I'm being robbed. It's those same ruffians from before!"

In the fading light, I saw him smile. Behind us,

shouts and pounding footsteps.

"We've got to go," John said.

"We need the Talisman!"

"He doesn't have it!"

"He must! He stole it!"

"We don't know that," John said. "All we know is he doesn't have it. And there are people after us."

We looked up the road. Four men, maybe five, running toward us.

"Come on," John said. He mounted the horse. "Climb up."

He helped us up, and with both me and Charlie sitting behind him, he made a wide path around Farran and continued down the road at a fast trot.

"Their stealing my horse," Farran shrieked.

"I think we need to trust Mr. Merwyn," Charlie said, as we bounced along.

"But we might find it."

"He told us to go home. We'll have another chance."

"If you can get home," John said.

The men were falling behind, but not by much. With the three of us on her back, the horse could barely go as fast as a running man. We trotted into the field with the group of men, shouting and waving various farm implements, not far behind.

We jumped off the horse and scrambled around the field.

"What are you looking for?" John asked, beginning to panic.

"Farran's cosh," Charlie said, sweeping his hands through the grass. "I buried it in the place where we arrived. We need to leave from the same spot."

John and I followed his lead, making broad circles

with our hands.

"Here," John shouted.

We ran to him as he pulled a cosh out of the dirt.

"Is this it?"

Charlie nodded. "Yeah."

We looked up. The men were getting closer.

"Do you have to be asleep under that cloak," John asked, "or do you just have to be unconscious?"

"Well, I'm not really sure," I said, "but …"

John grabbed the cloak from me and threw it over our heads. Everything went black and I bumped heads with Charlie as John pushed us together.

"Deep breaths," he said.

A strong arm wrapped around my chest. Beside me, Charlie began hyperventilating.

"That's it," John said, his voice next to my ear. "… six, seven, eight, nine …"

I rushed to catch up, breathing in double time.

"… ten. Now breathe in and hold it."

I filled my chest and felt John's arm squeeze. My ears buzzed, the darkness deepened, my head felt light, and then I was falling.

# Chapter 60
## Sunday, 9 July 2017 3:30am

# Charlie

I woke up with a headache and a sore chest, but I could tell immediately we were home. I was in a soft bed, and the air didn't smell like manure and mud.

I pulled the cloak off my face and looked at Mitch. "We're back," I said.

He looked around, blinking. "Yeah."

There wasn't much more to say about it. Mitch slipped off the bed and went out the door. As he did, I heard light footsteps in the hall. I panicked, but then realized they were heading away, toward our parent's room. Mitch looked at me, his eyes wide. When silence returned, I nodded, and Mitch opened the door. The hall was empty, except for the faint glow of the night-light.

Mitch went to his bedroom, taking the cloak with him, leaving me alone in the dark, wondering. Had Mom been outside my room, waiting and watching? And if so, what had she seen?

I decided it wasn't worth worrying about. I would never know, just as I would never know what happened to John, other than him becoming our great-great-great-great-grandfather.

# Chapter 61
## Thursday, 1 May 1851

# From the Diary of John Wyman

You'll think me insane, but I swear this is true. I found myself alone in the field, with my arms holding nothing but air. Until that moment, I had only half believed my friend's strange stories, but there was no denying the truth after that.

The farmers who old Farran had stirred up against us were almost on me. So much had gone wrong that week, most of it connected to Farran, that I didn't think adding horse thieving to the list would make much difference, so I mounted Vicky—that's what I eventually named the horse—and galloped away.

I rode right through the men who were chasing me, as Farran shook his fist and shouted, "Your life won't be worth a farthing when I get hold of you."

I had a good horse, nearly a hundred pounds in my pocket and a farm in Lancashire waiting for me. And if my mysterious friends were to be believed, I also had a long life and many descendants to look forward to.

I rode into the night, laughing.

# Historical Note

In her entry for the 1st of May 1851, Queen Victoria noted in her diary* "… the sight as we came to the centre where the steps & chair (on which I did not sit) was placed, facing the beautiful crystal fountain was magic & impressive …"

It seemed curious to mention the chair, and the fact that she did not sit on it. We now know the reason.

*http://www.queenvictoriasjournals.org/home.do

Likewise, the sale of the Crystal Palace, once the Great Exhibition was over, caused—according to historians—a bit of consternation within Parliament:

"… against the wishes of Parliamentary opponents, a consortium of businessmen, including Samuel Laing and Leo Schuster, who were both board members of the London, Brighton and South Coast Railway (LB&SCR), proposed that the edifice be relocated to a property named Penge Place …"*

Having read the account of Mitch and Charlie's adventure, we now understand how—and why—this opposition was overcome.

https://en.wikipedia.org/wiki/The_Crystal_Palace

## About the Author

Michael Harling is originally from upstate New York. He moved to Britain in 2002 and currently lives in Sussex.

Lindenwald Press
Sussex, United Kingdom

Printed in Great Britain
by Amazon